Murder in a
Pig's Eye

Murder in a Pig's Eye

LYNN HALL

A TRUMPET CLUB SPECIAL EDITION

Published by The Trumpet Club
666 Fifth Avenue, New York, New York 10103

ISBN 0-440-84104-6

This edition published by arrangement with
Harcourt Brace Jovanovich, Inc.

Printed in the United States of America
November 1992

10 9 8 7 6 5 4 3 2 1
OPM

1

Young Bodie Tureen was a fine broth of a lad, as they used to say in the old country, the old country in this case being Boston.

In the vast pressrooms of the *Boston Globe*, a middle-aged Irishman named Boris Tureen worked the inking machines and dreamed of the good life, away from the city. He dreamed of taking his family to the little village of Lower Bacpane in the Mahoosuc Mountains of New Hampshire. Boris had spent vacations in the valley as a boy, at an uncle's home where his girl cousin showed him things behind the barn that had nothing to do with farming. Happy childhood memories and the currently popular back-to-the-simple-life movement finally overcame Boris. He quit his job at the *Globe*, cashed in his insurance policies, and bought a tiny weekly newspaper in Lower Bacpane. He installed his wife and two small children in a huge old house at the edge of town, and they all lived happily ever after.

Young Bodie, the boy we started to discuss, had spent ten of his sixteen years in that old house at the edge of the village. It was home to him. He seldom noticed the good life all around him since he had little memory of any other kind.

He was a tall fellow, almost stout, with dark, soft straight hair, the candid gaze of a youth living the clean country life, and the first faint shadow of bankers' jowls. Puberty had been kind to his skin so far, and he had hopes of making it to manhood without the tiny volcanoes that decorated his friends' chins and cheeks. He was a bright, likable boy whose nebulous ambitions centered around living as comfortably as possible with the least physical effort.

So he greeted Gracie's plan with mixed feelings. Gracie was his younger sister, a plucked chicken of a girl whose scrawny shape and quick mind were a continual goad to Bodie. She was thirteen that summer and could outthink him as well as outrun him, keeping his position as alpha wolf in the sibling pack constantly under siege.

Gracie wore her hair two inches long. She cut it herself whenever it threatened to approach an attractive length. She backed up to the bathroom mirror and chopped off swatches of hair with her mother's sewing scissors until the top of her head was a sunburst of unruly tan spikes. She had sworn allegiance to horses over boys and was perhaps loading the odds against temptation with a hairdo only a horse could admire.

Gracie came home for lunch one day in mid-August and said to Bodie, "I've got a job for you. With pay. A real job."

Bodie looked at her askance, at least as askance as it was possible for him to look while eating macaroni and cheese. On days when Mrs. Tureen was helping out at the newspaper office, Bodie cooked lunch, and he always made macaroni and cheese, with extra cheese and extra pepper. The ecstasy of that cheesy sauce going down his throat was intense and almost blocked out Gracie's voice.

"Mr. Siler cut his arm on the chain saw," she said around a mouthful. "I was out there this morning sitting on Beauty, and he had this big bandage, and his arm was in a sling. I guess he cut it real bad. All the way down to the bone, and there was blood all over, and tendons hanging out, and . . ."

"Shut up. You're ruining my macaroni and cheese," he said.

"So anyway, Mr. Siler said he was going to hire some high school kid to work for him for a couple of weeks till his arm gets better. He'll pay minimum wage, and all you'd have to do is cut firewood and chore the livestock. I told him you'd do it," she said placidly.

"I don't know if I want to or not," Bodie said. He was irritated at her for offering him, and he was less than joyful at the prospect of two weeks of sweating in mosquito-filled woods running a chain saw that had already cut someone to the bone with blood all over and tendons hanging out. On the other hand, he'd just been moaning to Zach about the impossibility of earning car-buying money, and this job would possibly bring as much as three hundred dollars in just two weeks.

He smiled at the image of himself as a man of motored means. Then the smile widened at a new picture: Bodie Tureen, lean and hard from outdoor work, plaid shirt open down the front of his lean, hard body, girls lusting after him and eating him up with their eyes as he strode down the mountain trail, his killer chain saw swinging casually at his side.

"Another good thing," Gracie said in her dream-shattering voice, "Mrs. Siler won't be there. She's gone off somewhere. He won't say where she went, but he's a lot cheerfuler when his wife's not there, and he said she won't be back for a while."

It was a strong argument in favor of taking the

job. Bella Siler's absence was a good deal more inviting than her presence and would have been even to a stouter heart than Bodie's. His heart was one of the least stout parts of him.

Physical danger held no allure at all for Bodie Tureen. His job as assistant equipment manager was as close as he wanted to get to the great game of football, and he'd taken that job only because the school was so small that every boy had to do something. His choice had been between quarterback and assistant equipment manager.

Bella Siler didn't exactly spell physical danger, at least not anymore, but there had been the night a few years ago when he had climbed an elderly apple tree in the Silers' orchard on a dare, had split off a limb, and tried to nail it back into place. Bella had caught him in the act and chased him off the property with his own hammer brandished over her head.

"Okay," he said to Gracie. "I'll go out and talk to him about it this afternoon." Bodie had recently grown fascinated by instinctive decisions and the forces of fate behind them. If you walk home from school on Maple Street instead of Second because you had a sudden urge to, and on Maple Street you find a five-dollar bill blown up against the roots of a hedge, did you choose Maple because some mystic force knew about the fiver and wanted you to have it? Was it pure chance, or possibly an ESP force in your own head? On the other hand, how do you know that Second Street might not have yielded a ten-dollar bill?

This job that Gracie had just dropped on his foot, so to speak, had a feeling about it, Bodie thought. It had a feeling of potential excitement, as though something much bigger than minimum wages was waiting for him. Some memorable adventure.

His instincts were not far off target.

2

Henry Siler's farm was so small that it would have been called a hobby farm, or a gentleman's farm, if Henry had been a rich gentleman with time for hobbies. As it was, the Silers' forty acres was a leftover from another era, an almost self-sufficient small farm.

Henry raised a few acres of potatoes as a cash crop, grew out a steer a year for beef, kept a huge vegetable garden and a few old fruit trees and grapevines, raised two litters a year from an excellent Hampshire sow for pork and cash income. He heated his house with wood cut from his twenty acres of timber, and what he couldn't afford, he did without. This way of life suited him much better than it suited his wife, whose main arena of power was the Methodist Church. She could have ruled it more firmly with a better wardrobe of Sunday outfits.

From Bodie's house, which was the last house

on the south edge of town, you walked south on the main road a quarter of a mile, then turned right onto a small rock road, and Henry's was the first place on the right.

The Siler house sat close to the rock road looking picturesque and a little lopsided because one corner of it was sinking. It was a small frame house, two-storied but with low, cramped rooms and porches no sensible person would trust with his weight. Huge lilac bushes smothered the house at all its corners and covered some of the downstairs windows. The house had at one time been painted a mustard yellow. Not much of that paint was left, but the clapboard walls still gave off a creamy glow when the light was right.

Behind the house was a small barn leaning slightly toward the hillside and a scattering of other little outbuildings, all as innocent of paint as the barn. A wooded ridge rose beyond the house and buildings, extending northward from the road toward the town. Running clockwise from the road was the long wooded ridge, a fifteen-acre potato field at the base of the ridge, a small pasture and an orchard, then the road again, with the house and buildings in the center of the circle.

Bodie walked up the rock road that morning and approached the farmstead with a light step and a smile on his face. Mrs. Siler's absence had that effect on people.

Bodie followed the clang of a bucket and found Henry Siler in the pigpen awkwardly feeding his sow. Pouring out a bucket with only one hand is harder than it sounds.

Henry was a rounded sort of man, mid-height, his Oshkosh overalls well filled with belly. His skin was smooth and fine-grained, his pale eyes bland. Today his left arm rode in an impressive-looking black sling, from which his fingertips protruded pinkly. He stood up when he saw Bodie and smiled.

"Come to give me a hand, have you?"

"Or an arm," Bodie said. "The way Gracie tells it, you just about did yourself in with that chain saw. What'd it do, get away from you?"

"Aw, sprocket was getting worn, damn chain come off and whipped around and got me 'fore I could get clear of it. Now, what I need here is maybe four, five hours a day, mornings mostly. Feed and water the stock, clean the pens, then cut wood three, four hours. Come back for evening feeding, and that's it. Should be about two weeks till I'm out of this thing." He flapped the slinged arm. "Are you my man?"

"I'm your man," Bodie said with relish. "Gracie said your wife's gone someplace?"

Henry's expression went carefully blank. "That's right," he said shortly. "Here, take this bucket, get Gloria about half a bucket of that cracked corn over there in that bin."

"Gloria . . ."

"Gloria," Henry said as though talking to a fool. With his gaze he pointed toward the sow who stood close behind him, her snout busy with the table scraps he'd just dumped into her trough.

She was a fine figure of a pig, if you go for that sort of thing. She was black, with a broad band of white around her body. Like an Oreo cookie, Bodie thought. The arch of her topline was as high as his hip. Her neckless body was smooth and as firmly packed as the sausages that were her ultimate destiny. Tiny beady eyes were half hidden beneath the tips of her ears. Dainty cloven hooves splayed under the weight of her. At the far end of the blimp body, a stringy, kinky tail twitched with the joy of garbage in the trough.

"Gloria," Bodie said in affirmation. She ignored him.

"Granddaughter of the famous Perfection, greatest Hamp sow ever bred in this valley. Twice Grand Champion at the state fair. I loved her like a father. Perfection was the greatest pig I ever knew, and Gloria's dang near her equal. Well, don't just stand there admiring her beauty," Henry said. "My little girl is hungry. Hop to it."

Bodie hopped.

For the next hour Bodie worked while Henry leaned on fences and gates, telling him what to do and how to do it. Gloria's appetizer of table scraps and cracked corn was followed by an entrée of Sow Joy, Special Formula, because she was pregnant and needed babying. Her fall litters generally paid the property tax and the year's electric bills, Henry explained.

Then there were the two yearling steers in the barn lot to be fed, watered, and looked over. They seemed to lead a bored and boring existence.

In the small pasture behind the orchard lived the horse who drew Gracie to the farm for daily visits. Yellow Beauty was a large horse of a grass-stained cream color, with sleepy sunken eyes and a grotesquely drooping lower lip. She belonged to a married niece of the Silers' who had outgrown her interest in the horse but who didn't want to sell Beauty because the horse irritated her husband, and irritating him was one of the woman's few pleasures. Beauty had retired from a life of leisure to a life of near immobility, moving only as far as the next bite of grass.

All she required of Bodie was a few buckets of

water in the old clawfoot bathtub that had been thrown out when the house was remodeled forty years ago. It served now as a water trough.

Then there were half a dozen hens to feed and water. The hens seldom laid their eggs in their nest boxes because Henry thought it was cheaper in feed costs to let them run loose around the farmyard eating insects. Eggs might be laid in grass clumps along the yard fence, in the pile of old boots and harness bits in the corner of the barn, or in the front seat of Henry's Ford pickup if he left the windows rolled down.

At Henry's direction, Bodie played Easter egg hunt and managed to find two unbroken eggs. Henry seemed pleased.

It was midmorning before all the stock chores were done. Henry led the way into a small open-sided shed and pointed to a chain saw atop a rusted oil barrel. Its chain drooped off to one side, dried blood still brown on its steel teeth.

"There you go," Henry said cheerfully. "Just work that chain back over them sprocket teeth and you're in business. There's your gas can, there's your oil, there's your woods." With his good arm he waved toward the wooded slope behind the buildings.

Bodie looked at the saw but held back. "You

want me to use the same saw that just almost cut your arm off?"

"Course. It's the only saw I got."

Suddenly wishing he'd passed up this particular call of destiny, Bodie went forward reluctantly and picked up the saw. At the far end of the twenty-inch arm, he could see the wheel-like sprocket whose teeth moved the chain.

"I think that sprocket's shot, Henry," he said, just as though he knew what he was talking about. "Why don't I take the saw into town with me and have Eldon Perry take a look at it, maybe replace that sprocket. We don't want me ending up on the walking wounded list, do we?" He knew for sure *he* didn't.

Eldon Perry was a dried-up little old man with a Lincoln beard and a firm conviction that all the widows in town were after him with matrimony in mind. He lived his determinedly bachelor existence in a ramshackle house across the road from Bodie's and up a block toward town. Eldon had a workshop of sorts in the old barn-garage behind his house, where he tinkered happily with lawnmowers, chain saws, and an occasional vacuum cleaner.

He hoisted Henry's chain saw onto his workbench just inside the barn door and grunted over the removal of the worn sprocket. "Henry sent you out in the woods with this saw, might just as well shoot you."

"Dangerous, huh?" Bodie said.

"Might just as well shoot you. I hear he lost a good hunk of arm to it himself. That Henry ain't got the sense God gave a turnip."

Bodie grunted and found a relatively clean surface to prop against.

"Reckon Henry's missus had a few words to say on the subject," Eldon went on. "That Bella always did have a nonstop mouth. I think if I'd had to be married to that woman, I'd of sent her off to cut wood with a faulty chain saw, that's what I'd of done. You know, she used to be after me night and day, back when we was kids. She only married Henry because I was smart enough to see what it'd be like, living with a mouth like that."

Through Bodie's mind shot a flicker of connection between Henry's expression this morning, talking about his wife's absence, and what Eldon was saying. But it was only a flicker, and he shrugged it off. It was almost lunchtime by then, and the possibility of macaroni and cheese was a growing joy inside him.

". . . driving home from a dance in the old buckboard," Eldon was saying, "and she kept on grabbing at my knee. That woman never could keep her hands off me, I swear."

Bodie muttered sympathetically, "It's hell being a sex symbol."

"Sure is." Eldon sighed.

3

There was a lovely silence in the woods when the chain saw ran out of gas and coughed itself to death. Bodie set it on a stump and wiped his face against his arm, grateful for the breather. He had sawdust in his hair and eyelashes, and it gilded the sweaty streaks on his arms.

After lunch at home he had put on a thin plaid shirt. He'd begun a fantasy in which a beautiful girl who was visiting in the area got lost in Silers' woods and came upon this handsome plaid-shirted youth manfully manning the killer chain saw. She'd fall instantly and permanently in love with him, so that even if he said dumb things, she would think they were smart.

But lunch was three hours ago, and by now Bodie was hot and tired and sawdusty and in no shape to be fallen in love with. Luckily, it wasn't the girl of his dreams who came tromping up the hill from the road while he was drizzling oil into the saw. It was only Zach.

Zach Forth was a walking picture of rural New England youth, long and boney and lantern-jawed, with reddish hair and freckles even on his lips. He was handsome enough from the front, but in profile he was all nose and not much chin to speak of. His plan was to grow a beard just as soon as he had enough working beard follicles.

Zach had been drawn to Bodie Tureen sometime around fourth or fifth grade by the sense of freedom Bodie radiated. When Bodie had money, he spent it, a habit unheard of in the frugally Scottish Forth household. Bodie's family chatted and laughed and insulted one another, and food was plentiful. This aura of profligacy charmed Zach.

From his viewpoint, Bodie liked Zach for the simple reason that Zach liked him. For Bodie, that was usually reason enough to like anyone. And he was stimulated by Zach's imagination, which worked much like his own.

Through the woods ran a narrow timber road, just wide enough for Henry Siler's little old Ford tractor and its low-slung wooden dump cart. They were parked now near the stump where Bodie serviced the saw. Zach climbed the steep road and came to a stop beside the cart. He perched on its tire and leaned against its splintery flank.

"Working, I see."

"Hi. Yeah, Henry sliced himself up pretty bad on this baby"—Bodie manfully patted the saw—"so I said I'd help him out for a week or two, with chores and a little woodcutting. He's a neighbor . . ."

He made it sound like raising a barn for the widow and orphans, but Zach cut through the bull cookies. "He's paying you by the hour, right?"

"Well, yes, if you want to put it that way."

Zach grinned. He nodded toward the stump and said, "Looks like blood on there."

Bodie jumped back from the stump, then looked at it harder. He hadn't noticed the brownish streaks down the side of the stump, so subtly were they blended with the silver gray of the dead wood. He picked up the saw and studied the top of the stump, and with Zach squinting beside him, they traced a sizable bloodstain. It was almost invisible, having soaked down into the rough sawn surface of the wood.

"This must have been where Henry cut his arm," Bodie said, a little awed by the bloodstain. Blood-stains carried such an aura of murder mysteries about them.

Zach shook his head and frowned. "Too much," he said.

"What too much? Too much blood? You think this is too much blood for a cut on the arm? He's got his arm in a sling. Probably cut through veins and tendons and all that stuff, don't you think? That could cause quite a bit of blood to go spurting around, I bet."

Silently they stared around them, as though looking for more bloodstains on the trees and brambles.

Zach suddenly fixed a piercing eye on Bodie and said, "This looks like a murder spot to me. Is anybody missing? Who's the victim?"

"Oh, come on, Zach. Get real. Nobody's missing. Well . . . unless you'd consider Bella missing."

"Henry's *wife* is missing?" Zach's long face lit with the gory possibility. "Where does Henry say she's gone to? How long has she been missing? Why didn't you tell me?"

Bodie's eyes widened and met Zach's. "Henry didn't say."

Zach's eyes glittered.

"Why are you looking like that, Forth? What do you . . . oh . . . you don't . . . oh, come on. You don't really think . . ."

Zach raised one finely arched brow.

"Nah," Bodie said. "That doesn't happen in real life."

"In a pig's eye it doesn't," Zach snorted.

"What, nice old guys like Henry Siler offing their wives? Come on, don't give me that."

"Think about it," Zach said. "Think about living for forty years or whatever all alone on this lonely farm with . . . Bella." The name came out in a deep baritone.

The two looked at each other and thought about forty years of that mouth going at them all day, every day, do this, don't do that, give me this and that, get your feet off the furniture, don't eat that disgusting stuff.

That disgusting stuff was red licorice. It was well known around town that Henry Siler had a passion for red licorice and kept packets of it in the glove compartment of his pickup truck because Bella wouldn't let him eat it in the house. She said the smell of it made her sick, and it turned his teeth red.

"Yeah, but still," Bodie said after they'd both imagined the hell of living with Bella.

Zach began picking up cut lengths of firewood and tossing them into the cart. Bodie joined him.

"There was an old Alfred Hitchcock story on

television," Zach said, "about this mild-mannered New England farmer, just like Henry, and he had a bitchy wife, just like Bella."

"So? What'd he do?"

"Ground her up in the chicken feed. He had these prize chickens—his whole life was these chickens. He had his own feed grinder so he could make special blends of chicken feed. Chopped his old lady up and ran her through the blender and fed her to his hens."

"Oh, that's unreal," Bodie scoffed. "Nobody who cared that much for his chickens would risk throwing off their diets like that. Besides, how could you eat the eggs?"

"You're missing the point," Zach said, heaving an armload of elm chunks into the cart. "The point is, these mild-looking henpecked husbands . . ."

"Pun intended?"

"Shut up and listen. These are just the kind of guys who get fed up after forty years and off their wives."

"Well, Henry didn't," Bodie said stoutly. "Bella's alive and well and . . ."

"But you don't know where she is?"

"Well . . ."

"Henry didn't say anything about where she was?"

"No, just that she'd gone off somewhere, I guess. I didn't ask him. That was just what Gracie said."

Again Zach's arched eyebrow spoke volumes.

Bodie looked at him, wavered, and then said, "Naah . . ."

Zach helped wordlessly until the cart was loaded; then he jogged away down the timber road, across the fence, and into his father's pickup, which he'd parked beside the road. Thoughtfully Bodie wedged the chain saw into a firm perch atop the wood, lodged the gasoline can and plastic oil bottle into the load, and kicked the reluctant tractor into life. Before he pulled away, he stared another long, pondering moment at the blood on the stump.

He drove slowly up the hill to the turnaround clearing, then back down again, with the load lurching behind, into the farmyard. He stopped first at the toolshed to set down the saw and equipment, then backed the cart up to the woodpile against the north side of the house. Working with smooth, stomach-reducing bends and swoops, he stacked the afternoon's harvest of firewood in neat rows.

Henry was nowhere to be seen.

Bodie laid the last armload of wood on the stack and turned to wrestle the dump cart back to a horizontal position. A movement at the house window caught his eye, and he looked up. Henry stood within, smiling out at Bodie with red teeth. In his hand was clenched a whip of red licorice.

Bodie drove the tractor and cart into the shed, cut the ignition, and sat there with his arms resting on the steering wheel, his eyes gazing into excitement and adventure.

Could it be possible that crazy Zach was onto something?

Was Henry in there pigging out on forbidden licorice whips because he *knew* Bella would never again forbid him to eat them in the house?

Were red teeth his flag of victory over tyranny?

4

As Bodie carried buckets of dinner to Gloria, he saw his sister Gracie sitting on the horse. Beauty stood with sagging hip and drooping lip, her head hanging over the bathtub. Gracie sat backwards, a book opened on Beauty's boney rump.

When Gloria's trough was heaped with Sow Joy and her water barrel filled, Bodie brought water to the horse's bathtub. He stood watching, fascinated, while Beauty inhaled the water through her teeth, the pendulous lower lip drifting with the tide.

"Zach was looking for you," Gracie said, slamming her book and maneuvering into a forward position by flinging her legs precariously over the horse's rump and neck. Gracie's legs were long and lean and incredibly dirty.

"He found me."

"I told him you were up there cutting wood. You going home now? I'll go with."

They took Gracie's shortcut. Her natural instincts had shown her the most direct line to the nearest horse, a diagonal that crossed Beauty's pasture, a hayfield, a small stream, a field of tall weeds, and led into the southwest corner of the Tureen yard. It made little difference to Gracie that the barbed wire fence was tricky to climb, the hayfield rough to walk across, the stream just barely too wide to jump so that at least one shoe had to get wet, and the weed field an obstacle course of burrs and nettles. It was the most direct route from home to horse. Ten minutes of added travel time, a wet foot, and fifteen minutes of pulling cockleburrs from pants and socks was small price to pay.

If Bodie's mind had been with him, he would have vetoed the shortcut or left Gracie to trudge it alone, but in his bemusement he followed her, easing with exaggerated caution over the barbed wire and lifting his feet over the clumpy soil of the hayfield.

"Tell me again," he said, "what Henry told you about his wife. About where she went."

"He didn't say where, and I didn't ask him. It's just nice to be able to sit on Beauty without having her spying on me out the window and chasing me off. Old Henry, he doesn't give a fat rat who sits on his horse."

"But what exactly did he say? Did he say she'd gone off visiting, or what?"

Gracie shot him a look from her sharp little fox face. A tuft of hair stood upright from the back of her skull, like a rooster tail. "What's it to you, what he said? How come you're so interested all of a sudden?"

Bodie shrugged. "Oh, just something Zach said." The shrug fired up the aches in his back and shoulder muscles.

"What did he say?"

"Oh, nothing. Just he was telling me about some Alfred Hitchcock story about a farmer who murdered his wife and ground her up in the chicken feed. He was just being crazy."

They came to the stream. Gracie leaped with the grace of a steeplechaser. One foot slipped on the far bank and filled with water. Bodie went upstream a few yards, chose his spot with care, backed off and ran for it. His lead foot landed on an island hillock, which promptly crumbled under his weight. Both feet, one knee, and a hand came up wet and muddy.

They started into the weed field. Gracie said, "You mean Zach thinks Henry murdered Bella?" She sounded delighted at the idea, spooked in the pleasant way of ghost stories told in a safe house.

"Well, no, of course he doesn't really think

that," Bodie assured her. "He just sort of raised the question, and when I got to thinking about it, it seemed like old Henry was a little shifty-eyed when he told me Bella wasn't home. And then when I took the chain saw over to Eldon Perry's to get the sprocket replaced, Eldon made some stupid joke about Henry sending Bella out to cut wood with a lethal-weapon chain saw. It's nothing; it's just silly. Only it kind of stuck in my mind, and I thought maybe you knew where she really did go."

They walked single file on Gracie's private trail through armpit-high weeds. Gracie led the way, holding the weeds aside so that when she let go of them, they flailed Bodie with twice the power they would otherwise have had.

Gracie tromped silently for a while, then said, "If he did murder Bella, he'd have to go to jail for the rest of his life. So what would happen to all his animals?"

Bodie shrugged a shrug invisible to Gracie. "Sell them, I guess."

"I wonder if he'd give Beauty to me? Maybe if I asked him really really nicely, double please with cream and sugar on it, maybe he'd just give her to me, and I could still keep her at his farm."

"You're a ghoul. Did anybody ever tell you that?"

"Sure. I'm a ghoul. You're a boy." She did a hopping step that might have been a skip if the footing were better.

They emerged onto the mowed spaciousness of their own backyard and were not greeted by Sport, a middle-aged Chesapeake Bay retriever who lay in a shallow dirt wallow beside the back porch. Sport was large and swaybacked, with a coat of khaki curls and yellow eyes that glinted unpleasantly whenever they were open. Sport was a one-man dog; unfortunately, his one man had sold him to the Tureens and moved to Atlantic City to deal blackjack.

When Mr. Tureen moved his family to Lower Bacpane and the good life, his vision of the good life was clear and complete. It included a large old house with at least one fireplace, a spacious yard with shade trees, and a big dog who would lie at his master's feet in the evenings and go hunting with him on autumn weekends. Sport proved to be a dud at duck hunting because he refused to leap into icy water to retrieve shot ducks in spite of his breed's heritage for that sort of thing. And he never lay at his master's feet on winter evenings by the fire because his only recognized master was in Atlantic City dealing blackjack. Bodie's father couldn't quite bring himself to get rid of the dog, but the whole family had grown tired of being snubbed and were beginning to cheer each gray hair that appeared on Sport's muzzle. They wished him a painless old age and death . . . but the sooner the better.

Bodie and Gracie sat on the edge of the back porch and began pulling burrs from socks and pants legs. They untied their shoes, left them to dry on the porch, and padded into the kitchen.

Their mother looked them up and down and said, "Took the shortcut, I see. Gracie, you've got burrs on your shirttail still. You get all those burrs out before you put your clothes in the washer. I don't want those things snagging my good blouses."

She stood at the kitchen sink, ripping up fistfuls of lettuce. Glenda Tureen was an interesting-looking woman. You couldn't say pretty or cute or even attractive, but you could say interesting without stretching the point too far. She was short and squarely built, with a prominent forehead and a broad, square jaw. Her eyes were a faded gray green, rather small and deepset. Auburn hair hung in waves just to her ears in a style reminiscent of the roaring twenties, flappers, and the Charleston. The last time Glenda Tureen had worn makeup of any kind was at her husband's company's farewell party, the night before they left Boston for the good life.

Glenda Tureen had a secret longing. She wanted

to be a stand-up comedienne. She had neither the talent nor the looks for it and had never dared to try, even at school talent shows. But sometimes in the privacy of the bathroom, in front of the long mirror usually hidden by bathrobes and pajamas, she did a little bit of Joan Rivers or Lily Tomlin.

She had even named her daughter after her first heroine, Gracie Fields, although no one knew that.

While she built the salad and warmed a casserole in the microwave, her family gathered to lounge around the kitchen table in approved good-life style. Bodie's father sprawled at the table, scanning the evening *Globe* in search of typo errors that wouldn't have occurred if he were still working in the pressrooms. Boris Tureen was a big man, obviously Bodie's father, with dark Irish coloring, black hair, blue eyes, and red cheeks.

As Bodie sat down, his father said, "I heard you got a job out at the Silers'."

"Yeah, he hurt his arm, so I'm going to help out for a couple of weeks, choring and cutting wood."

"You be careful with that chain saw," Glenda said as she set the casserole on the table.

"I know. I am."

Chairs were scraped up into eating position, the evening *Globe* was laid aside, and for a few moments all mouths were busy eating.

Suddenly Glenda said, "Traveling salesman goes to this farm . . ."

Her family, who were used to her, prepared themselves.

"Salesman says to the farmer, 'Say there, I notice your pig has a wooden leg. What happened to it?' Farmer says, 'That there is a very special pig. He saved my life. Twice, he saved my life. Once the house caught fire and that pig came up under the bedroom window and made so much racket he woke up my wife and me. 'Nother time my tractor turned over on me, pinned me underneath. That pig rooted the dirt away till he'd dug me out. Saved my life.'

"Salesman says, 'Yes, but why does it have a wooden leg?' Farmer says, 'Listen, buddy, a pig that special, you don't eat him all at once.' "

She laughed uproariously, noticed she was laughing alone, and subsided. But Bodie, who was softhearted, threw her a grin to make her feel better.

5

The next morning Bodie was at the Silers' by seven, determined to get his three hours of woodcutting done in the morning, before sun and mosquitoes were at their worst. He Sow-Joyed Gloria, brought Beauty her bathtub full of water, played hide and seek with the laying hens, and was in the woods with cart and saw by eight.

The work seemed easier today. The aches gradually eased out of his muscles, and he began to enjoy the feel of the saw going through dead wood like a warm knife through butter.

By eleven he had filled the cart with freshly cut lengths, had hauled it down the hill, and was rhythmically stacking it behind the house. Most of the back wall of the little house had already disappeared behind the woodpile.

"Ah," Bodie thought as he tilted the cart bed back into place and drove the tractor toward the shed, "now home to lunch, hose off the sawdust, beat Gracie to the hammock, and read all afternoon." He loved to read, especially mysteries and detective stories. It was the best way he knew to live an exciting, dangerous life with no physical effort or risk whatsoever.

Henry sauntered out of the house and came to stand beside the growing woodpile, breathing red licorice breath and smiling in a saintly way at Bodie.

"You're doing a good job, young Tureen," he said. "Here, have a whip."

"You don't want it to get around town that you whip your employees," Bodie said with a straight face as he accepted the strand of candy. "You're hitting this stuff pretty heavy, aren't you? While the cat's away, the mouse is gorging on red licorice?"

He knew as soon as he said it that it was the wrong thing to say, calling Henry a mouse. But the man didn't seem to notice. He just smiled a rather vacant red smile.

"You might say that."

Bodie cleared his throat and tried for tact. "Where did you say your wife went to, Henry? I forgot."

Henry looked at him with amused scorn. "You didn't forget. I never told you."

"Yes," Bodie said pointedly, "I noticed that."

"Well, about time to start dinner," Henry said, turning to go.

"Henry."

"What?" A mite impatient now.

"Where is Bella? When's she coming back?"

"That's for me to know and you to find out. Only don't try. I didn't hire you to be nosy; I hired you to chore the stock and cut me some wood, and if you don't want to stick to the job, there's plenty of other kids around here."

Gracie came up beside Bodie and stared at Henry. Her bare legs showed dirty-horse marks from a morning of communion with Beauty.

As Henry disappeared into the house, she muttered, "Well, smell him. Who does he think he is, talking to you like that?"

"He thinks he's my boss, and he is. Come on, let's head for home."

This time they took Bodie's route, down the gravel road. They were still beside the Siler orchard when a dusty green Chevy pulled up beside them. Bodie and Gracie paused.

The window came down, and a woman's face appeared, a round, smiling middle-aged face set so low in the car that it obviously belonged to a shortie.

"Beg pardon," the woman said. "I'm looking for the Henry Siler place. He told me to turn right at the first road south of town, but silly me, I went right past this road and took that other one over yonder, and I didn't see any mailboxes that said Siler, although there was a Sylvester, so I thought to myself, I thought, I'll just bet you . . ."

"It's right over there," Gracie said, pointing to the mustard house behind the bushes. "Who are you?"

That was what Bodie wanted to ask but was too polite to blurt it out like that. Gracie had her uses.

The woman looked slightly startled, but answered cheerfully, "Why, I'm Henry's niece from Northwood, come to keep house for him while his wife's away."

Gracie gave Bodie a long, deep look. Aha, the look said.

"Well, thank you, children," the woman said, and disappeared behind the glare of her rolled-up window. The Chevy chugged off down the road and coasted into the farmyard.

Bodie and Gracie looked at each other. Without a word, they turned back and walked toward Henry's house. Henry emerged, grinning hugely, and started toward the woman, his arms open as if to hug her. But when he saw the Tureens standing near the mailbox watching, the hug became a sedate handshake.

"Althea, you're a sight for sore eyes. You found your way all right, I see. Here, let me get your bags. I was just getting out some baloney for lunch. Come along in." He threw a rather sharp glance at Bodie and Gracie and ushered the little woman into the house.

Bodie started again toward home and his own lunch, with Gracie bounding and cackling around him, jabbing at him.

"His niece," she hooted. "Who does he think he's kidding? That's his girlfriend if I ever saw one. Boy! Can you believe it? His wife's gone, what, two, three days, and here comes his niece, ho ho, moving in bag and baggage. Right in broad daylight, too."

"Oh, come on," Bodie said. "She probably is his niece. I mean, there are Silers all over this county. He probably has a truckload of nieces. Henry's wife goes off for the first time in her life to some unexplained destination which Henry refuses to talk about, and Henry's got his arm in a sling from what he says is a chain saw accident, so he probably does need someone to cook and keep house for him. Even though he's been doing okay so far, cooking with one hand and letting the house go dirty. . . . I think it's perfectly logical that he'd get some . . ."

"Swinger," Gracie offered.

"Some respectable-looking middle-aged lady relative to come in and . . ."

It sounded weak, even to him.

Gracie scoffed. "Middle-aged to us, maybe, but to an old boot like Henry, that woman probably looks like the breath of spring. Especially when you put her up against old Bella Badmouth."

Bodie's walking speed picked up as his thoughts gathered velocity. If Henry really was moving a tootsie into the farmhouse, under the pretense that she was his niece, come to keep house for him temporarily, that might mean that he knew something no one else knew. It might mean that he knew he was safe from Bella because Bella was dead. Ground up for chicken feed?

Oh come on, he scoffed at himself. This was just stupid. Impossible. Henry was a nice old guy who wouldn't hurt anyone. Just a nice old guy with blood all over his elm stump, a sling that might or might not be genuine, and an awfully big smile of welcome for his—ho ho—niece.

After lunch Bodie found that he couldn't get into his library book. He lay, all fed and showered, in the hammock with his book against his knees and all afternoon to enjoy it, but his eyes kept unfocusing. When a man is living on the dangerous edge of a real-life murder mystery, the printed page pales.

After a while he got up and walked downtown with Gracie trailing after him. He got the car keys from his father on the firm promise to have the car back by five.

It was a seven-year-old Country Squire station wagon, boring white in color, with wood-grained side panels and the fragrance of wet dog inside. The family had no particular use for a station wagon, but it fit Boris Tureen's vision of himself as country editor, sportsman, and liver of the good life. Bodie's self-image ran more to the luxury of a Mercedes.

Gracie sprawled on her stomach in the cargo area behind the backseat. Her parents never let her ride that way for fear she'd shoot out through the back window head first in case of an accident. But Bodie didn't much care how she rode. He didn't plan to have an accident between here and Zach's place.

The Forth farm was three miles north of town on the main highway. It was tidy in an efficient way, no space wasted on flower beds. It was primarily a dairy farm, milking an average of fifty good Shorthorns. There had been several Forth children, but most were grown now and escaped to easier lives elsewhere.

Late August was a relatively slow time here. In a week or so the last cutting of hay would be ready to harvest, but for now the six hours a day of milking, feeding, and manure-hauling were the primary jobs, and they were done mornings and evenings.

Bodie found Zach near the main machinery shed, perched on the concrete foundation of a former building. Ordinarily Gracie would have gone looking for Zach's sister Sarah, who was only eleven but better company than the boys, in Gracie's opinion. But today she stuck beside Bodie. This was where the good action was going to be today.

"Whatcha doing?" Bodie asked, dropping down onto the concrete rim beside Zach. Behind them and shading them, the machine shed was long enough to house a Third World nation. The dairy barn was to their right in a clutter of lesser buildings, and the farmhouse sat before them, across a stretch of seldom-mowed lawn. Mr. Forth didn't believe in wasting gas money on lawnmowers, and he was running out of children young enough to be browbeaten into pushing the ancient reel mower around the yard. Mostly they just depended on feet to wear down the grass.

"Waiting for Dad to get back from town," Zach said. He motioned to the mammoth hay mower-conditioner that stood just inside the building. "Sheared a bolt on that sucker. Have to get a replacement. What are you guys up to?"

"Our armpits," Gracie said dramatically, "in murder and adultery."

Zach's mouth twitched. "Which one are you doing, Gracie?"

"No, seriously," she insisted. "Listen, Henry Siler has got this actual broad living with him. No lie. She moved in this morning. We saw her, didn't we, Bode? You tell him."

In his role as sensible older brother Bodie said, "Well, I don't know that I'd call her a broad exactly."

"Well, you couldn't call her a narrow," Gracie yelped. "You saw the hips on that . . ."

"That's not the point," Bodie said, and turned to Zach. "This strange woman did move in with him, though. She said she was his niece from someplace or other . . ."

"Northwood," Gracie offered.

"Whatever. She looked like she was in her forties, so she could be a niece. I'd guess Henry is, what, early sixties? He could have a niece in her forties in Northwood."

"Or . . . not," Zach said thoughtfully.

Gracie blurted, "She's not his niece. I could tell from the way they looked at each other when she got out of the car. Old Henry started to grab her; then he saw us standing there, and he real quick sort of dropped his arms. Guilty like, if you ask me."

Zach lifted one eyebrow and said, "Blood on the stump."

"Come on, you guys," Bodie argued. "Even if she is his . . . broad or whatever, that doesn't mean he necessarily did anything to Bella. He might have just sneaked this girlfriend in for some messing around while Bella was gone to . . . wherever . . ." He was trying to be sensible, but the excitement of the idea was getting to him.

"But why won't he tell us where Bella is?" Gracie said. "You and I both have tried to get it out of him, and he acts funny. Guilty. Tells us to mind our own business. This morning he even threatened to fire Bodie if he didn't quit asking about Bella. Now if that's not acting guilty, I don't know what is."

"Okay," Zach said, "if he killed her, what did he do with the body?"

The three of them stared at one another, their minds scanning the Siler farm.

"Could have buried her," Bodie said. "Except, where? There aren't any dug-up places on the farm, no fields under cultivation this time of year. The hayfield's covered with hay. The garden is covered with beans and tomato plants."

Zach opened his mouth, but Bodie interrupted. "And no, Henry doesn't have a grinder for his chicken feed. He buys plain old scratch from the feed mill."

Gracie, who was too wired to sit down, bounced before them, her rooster tail of hair flopping atop her head. "Let's search the place and find the body. Well, maybe not you, Zach. You wouldn't have any reason to be there, but Bodie and I sure do. I'm over there all the time sitting on Beauty. Henry never even notices me. And, Bodie, you could look all over that whole woods while you're supposed to be cutting wood."

Bodie pondered. What if Henry really did murder his wife? It would be sickening if they actually did find her body. But on the other hand, it would make Bodie a hero for life around Lower Bacpane. Any girl he wanted, he could get. He probably wouldn't even have to lose weight.

And the sheer excitement of it! Matching wits with Henry Siler. Bodie knew he could do it with one wit tied behind his back. And after all, it was only forty acres. How many hiding places could there be on a farm that small?

6

Thousands, Bodie realized the next day as he stood looking around the farmstead, a bucket of Sow Joy stretching each arm. Thousands of places on a forty-acre farm that could hide a body. Dig a grave in the woods and cover it with leaves. Or in the garden between tomato plants, or in one of the old sheds under a pile of junk.

It was Sunday, so he was doing only the necessary feeding chores that day and had no excuse to be in the woods. This would be thinking day, he decided. Reconnoitering day. Time to use his head, put himself in the criminal's place, and decide what he would do with a two-hundred-pound dead wife.

The woods really were the most logical hiding place, he decided as he dumped Gloria's breakfast into her trough and scratched the summit of her back for her. Bare grayish skin showed through the sparse bristles of hair on her shoulders. Gloria huffed into her Sow Joy and leaned against Bodie's scratching hand, almost toppling him with her weight.

"She's a glorious creature, ain't she?" Henry appeared beyond the fence, apparently enjoying the sight of someone else doing his work. "That's how come I named her Gloria. Ma thought it was for Gloria Vanderbilt, but naturally that was foolish."

"Naturally," Bodie agreed.

"Gloria Vanderbilt don't look nothing like my little darlin' here. Those racy lines, that elegance through the head. And just look at the size of them feet. Just like old Perfection."

"No mere woman could compare," Bodie agreed. "What did your wife think about Gloria?" he asked, innocently inserting the past tense "did" as a trap.

Henry tensed up and gave Bodie a split-second squint. "Bella likes to spend money, and Gloria has twelve to a litter twice a year. That answer your question?"

The house door slammed, and Althea came out into the sunlight, dressed in flowered polyester and white high-heeled shoes. She picked her way across the dirt yard and stopped several yards short of

Gloria's domain. After a brief smiling nod toward Bodie, she said, "Are you sure you won't change your mind and come along, Henry? I'd love to have you."

I'll bet you would, Bodie thought. He smiled blandly and went on scratching Gloria.

"Nah," Henry said. "That much sitting on those hard pews would make my arm hurt. You go on and enjoy yourself. Two blocks north of the Amoco station. You can't miss it."

Bodie and Henry leaned on the pigpen fence from opposite sides and watched Althea drive away toward town and the ten o'clock service at the Trinity Methodist Church. Bodie thought, Good move, guys. Althea goes to church, gets acquainted, makes a good impression on people, gets public opinion on her side. If they'd both gone to church together, it would have looked too brazen. This way, she's just the respectable middle-aged niece, come to keep house for Henry while his wife's away and his arm is laid up. Good maneuver, Henry.

As Henry straightened up and showed signs of shuffling off, Bodie grabbed at him with a conversational fishhook. "Is Althea married, Henry?"

Henry shot him another slit-eyed look. "What makes you ask that?"

Bodie shrugged. "Just wondered. She seems like a nice lady. I just wondered if she had family, or what."

"She's a widow."

Henry sounded a little prickly on the subject. Bodie's instincts stood at attention. "Oh, that's too bad. When did her husband die? What did he die of?"

"How should I know? Them calves is hungry. You better get on with your chores. I'm not paying you to stand around."

The Tureens had a ten o'clock Sunday brunch as they usually did. Then Glenda drove Gracie and two of her friends over to High Bacpane, to the municipal swimming pool so that Gracie could ignore the boys there.

She'd made a pact with her best friend Kari that whichever one of them first deserted horses in favor of boyfriends would never be spoken to again by the other. This pact had been painless enough when they were eleven and were in absolutely no danger of attracting boyfriends. But by now, at thirteen, Kari was showing definite signs of pact-breaking, which made Gracie more grimly determined than ever to be true to the pact and to hold Kari to it.

His mother invited Bodie to go along, but he

opted out. For one thing, Kari had begun to shoot flirting looks at him behind Gracie's back, and he never knew how to respond. It was better to be flirted with than not, he supposed, but when the flirter was of no interest to the flirtee at all, then it got embarrassing. Bodie had babysat with Kari and her younger sister when he was thirteen and desperate for spending money. He had seen her spit in her sister's hair to even the score over a video game. It was hard to feel romantic about someone after a thing like that.

He had other reasons for declining the swimming trip. He didn't like the way he looked in swim trunks, with that little white roll of fat that rode just above the trunks. And there was the ever-present danger that some girl would look up the legs of his trunks and see something embarrassing.

Swimming in municipal pools was highly over-rated anyway, he thought. Too crowded, too noisy, too sunny. Later on in his life he planned to be rich enough to have a private pool with landscaping and shaded lounge chairs. Till then he could do without swimming.

He spent the afternoon lying on the living room floor watching baseball with his father. Boris wasn't actually watching; he was slowly devouring the Sunday *Globe*, the *Times*, and the *Chicago Tribune*. The baseball game merely made pleasant background music.

It took an effort of will for Bodie to get himself up at four o'clock and to leave the window air conditioner for the heat and dust of the Siler farm. But duty called. Gloria's trough was once again empty of Sow Joy, and there was brainwork to be done.

Althea's Chevy was in place beside the house, but Henry's pickup was gone when Bodie arrived. He fed and watered and found three hen eggs in a rubber overshoe in the junk pile behind the machine shed. He took the eggs into the kitchen, where Althea was breading pork chops for supper.

"Eggs," Bodie said, showing them to her and setting them in the wire basket in the pantry.

"Thank you, um . . ."

"Bodie," he supplied.

"Oh yes. Bodie."

"Henry gone somewhere?" Behind her back Bodie stared at the plump little woman, trying to imagine her and Henry naked together. Impossible. The mental picture just wouldn't come.

Althea looked at him over her shoulder but went on patting her chops. "He went fishing."

"Oh. I guess you can fish one-handed."

"Evidently so."

"How was church?" Bodie asked, settling himself against the refrigerator door for a long visit.

"Oh, fine." She smiled. "You've got a lovely minister in Reverend Tule. Such a kind man. Such an understanding man. It was a lovely service, although I do think a church service ought not to have quite so much modern music. I mean, what's wrong with 'Rock of Ages,' or 'Holy, holy, holy, Lord God Almighty, All Thy works shall praise Thy name in earth and sky and sea . . .'"

She warbled up into song.

Feeling that it was time to break in, Bodie broke in. In fact, he wondered whether she ever actually stopped speaking of her own volition, or just went on until somebody interrupted her.

"Do you go to church back home, you and your husband?" He felt a bit mean, introducing the sad subject and pretending he didn't know about her widowhood, but her singing voice had the quality of a rusty saw against a pine knot, and it needed cutting off quickly.

"My husband's deceased." Althea dropped instantly from earth and sky and sea into widowhood. "He was a pillar of our church, rest his soul. He raised the funds for the new septic tank almost single-handedly. Pity he wasn't such a good provider for his own nearest and dearest. Rest his soul."

"Amen," Bodie said foolishly. But Althea accepted it as the proper response. "How did he . . . ?"

Althea dropped her chin sadly, making a triple-decker out of it. "Corn picker got him."

"Ah," Bodie said. "I'm sorry. That must have been terrible for you."

"Yes. It was. Wasn't no picnic for him, either."

Althea talked on about how good the neighbors had been to her and how many casseroles showed up on the day of the funeral, but Bodie wasn't listening. He was wondering about the coincidences here, first Althea's husband dying a violent death, then Henry's wife mysteriously disappearing, then, presto, Althea and Henry living together. It looked pretty suspicious to him.

The kitchen clock, shaped like a frying pan, said ten till six. Bodie said, "Say, do you mind if I turn on your television for a minute? I want to catch the baseball score." He hadn't even paid attention to the baseball score when he was watching the game, and he certainly wasn't interested in it now, but it was an excuse to poke through the house.

Althea nodded toward the living room but stayed at the stove, where the pork chops were now tanning themselves in the skillet.

Bodie turned on the television to make it look

good, then stared around the room, absorbing possible clues.

It looked like a clueless room to him on the surface of things. But he knew from all his reading that the best detectives absorbed the personalities of their suspects by studying every detail of their lives, and clues presented themselves in the most innocent places.

This was a boring living room. It was small and square and barely comfortable. Two windows and a door let in heat in the summer and, Bodie guessed, drafts in the winter. A brown oil stove sat in one corner and an elderly RCA floor-model television in another. On the floor there was an elderly gray carpet sculptured in a swirl pattern that was supposed to make it look expensive but failed. The sofa was two pieces of a tan sectional. The corner section stood alone as a wedge-shaped chair without the comfort of arms. A white metal table shaped like a circular staircase held dusty plants of the kind old ladies grew. African violets, Bodie thought they were. They needed watering.

A clue? Would a woman who cared about her plants just go off and leave them to die of thirst? Or was it just that Henry was falling down on the watering?

Atop the television set were a clutter of photographs in cheap frames, wedding and graduation pictures, and a snapshot of a younger Henry standing in front of an apparently new De Soto sedan.

Bodie found a picture of several family members of mixed generations sitting on a sofa beside a Christmas tree. There was Henry, and there was Bella looking not at the camera but down at a toddler who appeared to be driving a toy race car up her leg.

Adjectives like "stern, imposing" came to Bodie's mind as he studied the face. It was built of strong, mannish features, a nose too large for a woman and ears noticeably long and outstanding. Her hair was in a long braid wrapped about the crown of her head in a style almost never seen anymore.

Her bosom was shelved out and held in place by miracles of Playtex that Bodie could only wonder at. He wondered, too, how anyone built like that could have any sort of contact with her feet. Trying to imagine her naked was even more impossible than Althea and Henry had been, maybe because she was not only old and big, but majestic as well.

Hanging on the wall over the television was a framed photograph of Henry grinning over the back of a huge black and white sow. Over the sow's back was draped a purple Grand Champion rosette. This had to be the famous Perfection. Bodie squinted up close to the picture, looking for a family resemblance with Gloria. If there was one, he wasn't pig man enough to see it.

From the kitchen Althea's voice went on. Bodie heard the voice, but not the individual words, until Althea appeared in the doorway saying, ". . . doesn't get back pretty soon, supper's going to be late. I want to get out of the kitchen by seven, you know. Got to watch 'Murder, She Wrote.' Don't you just love the way Jessica always knows who did it before anyone else? I just think Jessica is wonderful. It's so nice to have a mature woman as a star instead of all those silly young things with mops of hair and high boots and . . ."

"Well, I better get on home," Bodie said, backing out through the living room door.

Walking up the gravel road toward town, he thought, If Henry did away with Bella because she got on his nerves talking all the time, and if he thinks this new one is going to be any better, ho ho, lots of luck, Henry. Still, they say people tend to marry the same types over and over, even if they can't stand that type.

The day hadn't given him much in the way of proof of murder, nor of ideas as to where the body might be. But tomorrow would be better, he thought. Tomorrow he'd have all morning to search the woods, under cover of cutting wood. And Gracie would look for fresh graves in the horse pasture while she sat on Beauty.

Tomorrow things would get rolling.

He pictured himself finding dug earth in the woods and leading the police to it. The scene skipped over the gory part and shifted directly to the television interviews and the first day of school, when he'd be surrounded by girls wanting to get close to the hero; girls who might have spit in their sisters' hair but not in Bodie's presence. Romantic girls.

He sighed and probed his waist to see if the bulge was still there. It was.

Bodie rushed through the feeding chores the next morning and was in the woods before seven-thirty. He'd hoped to get past the house and onto the ridge without catching Henry's attention, so that he could have extra time for searching and still finish his three hours' worth of sawing before lunch. But the tractor was noisy, and Henry had peered out at him from the kitchen window as he'd rattled past.

The timber road ran the length of the ridge, along its summit. There was a turnaround loop at the far end and a few short spur tracks here and there, where the woodcutting had led the tractor into the brush. It was a mixed timber, oak and ash and a few patches of small pines. The oaks were fairly clean underfoot because their blankets of fallen leaves discouraged undergrowth, but the ash groves and the small clearings, where heavy cutting had been done years ago, were grown up heavily with bramble thickets, wild berries and prickly ash, and other impenetrable growth.

Bodie drove the full length of the ridge, circled the turnaround, then parked the tractor and began walking toward the fence that marked the edge of the woods and of Henry's land. If I were burying a body, he thought, I'd get it to the farthest spot I could from where I lived.

He studied the ground, looking for disturbed earth. Casting from side to side like a bird dog, he covered the far corner area and circled back toward the tractor, avoiding only the places too brambly for him or Henry to have walked through.

He found no graves, but he did come across a pair of young ashes blown over by a storm and long dead. He started the saw and worked up the trees; then he started off in another direction, scanning the ground with an eagle eye. He decided to do it methodically, marking a certain tree or bush, lining it up with another marker, and covering that territory thoroughly before moving on to the next eye-marked section.

He had covered all of the territory between the turnaround and the end of the woods and was working his way southward, eagle-eyeing left and right, when suddenly he gasped and froze.

Henry stood uphill from him, watching him with a hard, cold eye.

Bodie felt himself go red, then pale. For the first time he realized that a man who has killed once will kill again, especially if he thinks someone is onto him. Henry stood beside the tractor cart, one hand resting just inches from the chain saw.

Bodie's legs turned to water.

"What you looking for down there?" Henry asked in a smooth voice that clashed with the steel in his eyes.

Bodie forced his lips upward into a smile. "Oh, Henry. You gave me a scare. I was just . . . uh . . . taking a little bathroom break." He chuckled man-to-manfully.

"Well then, you must be the most gawdamn modest feller in the world. You been walking from tree to tree for twenty minutes looking for your spot. What's the matter—afraid the squirrels will see you?"

"Oh. Well. Heh, heh, no, uh, I did that already. I was just looking around for, well, you know, uh, dead trees. To cut up."

Henry's eyes squinted up into evil slits. "Don't give me that cow flop. I'm not paying you good money to wander around up here; I'm paying you to cut wood."

"Yes, sir." Bodie had never said sir in his life before, but it seemed appropriate now.

"And furthermore than that," Henry said as he turned to walk away, "I know what you're hunting, and you ain't going to find it up here."

Bodie stared after him.

The saw roared, chips flew, and lengths of truncated branches fell to the ground in a neat row as Bodie worked his way up a length of fallen oak limb. Work fast, keep an eye peeled for Henry, and make quick trips into the woods on either side of the timber road, eagle eyes darting. That was the master plan, conceived and carried out by a shaken master.

"I know what you're hunting, and you ain't going to find it up here." That was proof. Henry really had done in his wife, and he knew Bodie was onto him.

There was a threat implied in Henry's words. Bodie recognized it and cowered before it. But a good detective never gives in to veiled threats; he just becomes more cunning.

In the back of his mind an indistinct fantasy was crystalizing: the world-famous Boris Tureen the Second dwelt high above Boston in a fabulous penthouse and solved unsolvable crimes with his steel-trap mind. He had a young assistant with a name like Archie who did all the legwork and research, while the great Tureen sat in his easy chair by the marble fireplace and worked out the obscure clues in his head. He had some exotic hobby, like growing orchids, a cook who made cordon bleu macaroni and cheese, and so many beautiful women falling in love with him that it got boring.

The fantasy was so much fun to think about that he had to force himself to concentrate on the murder beneath his nose. His mind was much happier frolicking through daydreams than it was focusing on dead bodies underfoot and threats from a homicidal maniac who looked like Grampa on the Farm.

After Henry's parting shot, "I know what you're hunting," there could be little doubt that Henry had indeed done in Bella. What had started as a game was suddenly an undertaking in dead earnest. So to speak. Henry had killed and might kill again. He had to be caught and brought to justice, and in order to do that, Bella's body would have to be found. And who was in a better position to look for it than Bodie Tureen?

The saw ran out of gas and died. With relieved back muscles Bodie stood upright and set the saw on the cart's tailgate to cool before refilling it. He looked down through the tree branches and saw Henry's red shirt near the barn. Furtively Bodie made another loop through the woods, searching.

Nothing. No graves, no telltale scraps of women's clothing on brambles. He went back to oil and gas the saw. "You ain't going to find it up here," Henry had said, as though they were playing a game of hide and seek. Was it a game in Henry's mind? Was he one of those psycho cases who wants to be caught? Or was he trying to discourage Bodie from further woods searches because that's where the body really was?

Why hire me at all? he pondered suddenly. If he'd just murdered his wife and hid the body somewhere on the farm, why hire a neighbor kid who might find it?

Maybe because he didn't figure the kid was terribly bright.

Maybe because he really did need the help. He heats that house completely with wood, and that means a lot of stockpiling before winter. And it is hard to do the animal chores with one arm.

For the rest of the morning Bodie alternately sawed as fast as he could and made quick side trips through the trees and brambles. By eleven-thirty he had a full load on the cart, no grave discoveries in the woods, and not a centimeter of unscratched skin on his forearms.

Whatever Henry's reason for saying "You ain't going to find it up here," it was beginning to look like a true statement. Wherever Bella's body was, Bodie was reasonably sure it wasn't on the wooded ridge.

So, what next? he asked himself as he offloaded the wood behind the house. No answers came to mind. But from the kitchen window Althea twinkled her fingers at him, and from the living room window Henry watched and chewed red licorice.

Bodie, alias Boris Tureen the Second, dined that day with BT the First at the Koffee Kup Kafe across the street from the newspaper office. He'd gone home first, showered off the sawdust, and finding neither sister nor Kraft Dinner in the house, had wandered the two blocks up the street to the newspaper office.

Bodie enjoyed these dad-and-son lunches. He knew his father liked to pretend the two of them were business partners doing lunch: Tureen and Son, Publishers. He hadn't yet mentioned to his father that his dreams lay elsewhere, that the bright city lights beckoned him away from the good life. Time enough for disillusioning his father later. For now, he needed to pick his father's brain, painful though it might sound.

They took a booth by the front window, so Boris could wave at people going by. He was a big man, like Bodie would be, and stomachs were a bit of a problem in close-fitting booths like this one, but the flesh got settled somehow and the orders given. Hoagie with onion rings and coffee for Boris, cheeseburger with fries for Bodie.

Boris wore a slightly rumpled white shirt with the collar open. His tie was pulled loose, and a sweater vest hung unbuttoned because it would no longer stretch over the Tureen prow. Although he looked as though he'd been dressed by the director for a movie part as small-town newspaperman, there was also a quality of genuineness about the man that even his son recognized. Boris was exactly what he labeled himself, and if the labeling had taken place after forty years of living a different life, it was no less genuine, no less in keeping with the essence of the man. He was and always had been a small-town newspaperman by nature, even during the lost years in Boston. He was genuinely interested in who had Sunday dinner with out-of-town relatives and whether it was financially feasible to run sewer lines out Wilson Road.

"Dad," Bodie said, "have there ever been any murders around here that you remember? I mean, like, you know, domestic violence."

"Murders?" Boris didn't seem especially surprised by the question. Newspapermen dealt with such things as routine stuff. "Not right around here that I can think of. An occasional wife-beating, maybe. And the time what's-his-name Robertson caught his wife in bed with his brother-in-law and chased him naked through an oat field shooting bird shot over his head."

"No, I mean, say, if somebody was going to murder someone on, say for instance, an old farm out in the country, where do you think would be a good place to hide a body?"

"You planning to do somebody in, are you?" His father's eyes twinkled.

Lunch arrived, and for a few minutes the cheeseburger took precedence over everything else. It had been a very long time since breakfast.

"No," Bodie said finally, when the last scrap of lettuce was gone and he'd begun poking fries into the ketchup pool at the side of the basket. "I was just . . . thinking about writing a murder mystery, and I was trying to think of good hiding places for a dead body. I wanted to be as authentic as possible, and I just thought you might remember some famous case that was in the news years ago, or something."

Boris accepted this explanation. Bodie had always been a reader and had exercised his imagination from a very early age.

"Hmm, let me think. I remember one deal, right after we moved up here. I don't recall the names now, but somebody bought an old farm up north a ways. Buildings had been abandoned for years. There was an old cistern beside the house. The new owners wanted it filled in for some reason or other, and when they opened it up, they found a human skeleton down in there. It was a woman's skeleton. Checked back and found out that the last person to live there was a crabby old bachelor who'd lived with his sister. It was her farm, I guess, inherited from her husband who'd died years before. The neighbors said the brother and sister never got along, and she disappeared finally. He told people she'd moved to Florida. Nobody ever saw reason to check up on it, and by the time they found the body, the old man was long dead himself. So they never looked into it any farther than that."

Bodie stared, his mind racing. It did happen, then. People did murder one another on lonely farms and get away with it. Fifty years from now, Bella Siler's remains might come to light, decades after Henry and Althea lived happily ever after.

Or would Althea disappear too, a few years down the road when Henry got tired of listening to her?

Get away with it once, do it again.

Bodie shivered. He tried to think whether there was a cistern at Henry's house. There was a square concrete platform at the side of the house with a concrete disk on top, and sitting on the disk was an antique milk can planted with neglected-looking marigolds. That was probably an old cistern, and that was possibly . . .

Henry would have heard the story of the old dead guy and the skeleton in the cistern. A story like that would cover the county like a snowfall. Henry might have been thinking about offing Bella ever since he heard that story, thinking about it every time she crabbed at him for something or took his red licorice away from him. The idea grew in Henry's mind until enough time had passed that he felt safe in copying the other man's successful plan. He spent years perfecting the details, and when the time was right, wham. No more Bella. A perfect crime, already proven successful by that other guy.

Hah, Henry. Not quite perfect. That other man didn't have Bodie Tureen to deal with.

Cistern, here we come.

Bodie's bedroom seemed to reflect less individuality than most teenaged boys' rooms. The bed was made; there were no posters of rock stars on the walls, no clutter of scientific apparatus or sports equipment, or even dirty clothes.

But these minuses in themselves were a portrait of the inner Bodie Tureen. He made his bed as soon as he was out of it every morning simply because he loved the luxury of slipping into a smooth envelope of sheets at night, and he knew no one else was going to make his bed for him if he didn't.

He didn't keep posters of rock stars because, for one thing, he didn't especially like rock music, although he'd have ripped out his tongue by the roots rather than confess that dislike to any of his friends. He had a hard enough time being one of the guys without having it known that he was a closet Rachmaninoff lover. Then, too, he wasn't a worshiper by nature. He had a hunch that behind the wild clothing and green hairdos of the electric music-makers were small people who were very probably not worth worshiping if you knew what they were really like. He'd have enjoyed hero-worshiping someone, but he was holding off for somebody genuinely worth it.

Neither science nor sports were his fields, either. Books were, head games were, solving puzzles and getting lost in stories or daydreams were, and his bedroom was an accurate reflection of the real him.

It was a large room, with a slanting ceiling along one side, and a dormer window with a cushioned window seat. The rugs were hand-braided by Grandma Tureen, multicolored and thick. The bed and dresser were bird's-eye maple, and the bedspread was a quilt.

If the room was a shade too self-consciously country New England, Bodie didn't notice. He liked it. He enjoyed imagining himself a successful man of forty, living in his tastefully elegant penthouse and looking back with pleasant nostalgia on his boyhood bedroom. The maple furniture and braided rugs were just right for that sort of nostalgia.

Sometimes if he was expecting friends, he unmade the bed and threw clothes around, so that he wouldn't be suspected of being a neat-freak. But tonight Zach had caught him unprepared, and the room was tidy.

Gracie lay belly-down across the bed. Bodie's long legs were curled into the window seat embrasure, and Zach was sprawled half on the beanbag chair, half on the rug. Zach was a floor-sitter by nature.

"So that's what I think happened," Bodie said, winding down. "I think old Henry heard that story, too, just like Dad told me, and he killed Bella and dumped her in the cistern. You've heard of copycat crimes. They talk about them on television all the time, how one person, like Jack the Ripper, does some special kind of crime, and then other people do the same thing. I'll bet you anything that's what Henry did. Put her down the cistern."

"What's a cistern?" Gracie asked belligerently. She hated not knowing something Bodie knew.

"It's the opposite of brethren," Bodie said. "Brethren and cistern, we are gathered here today to pray for the soul of . . ." His voice and arms rose like a television minister's.

"It's an underground concrete tank," Zach said. "For holding rainwater."

Bodie said, "They used to have them beside old houses. The rainwater would come down the roof, go into eave spouts, then down a drainpipe into the cistern."

"Why?" Gracie asked.

"Well water was hard," Zach said. "That was before water softeners were invented. Well water had iron in it, and it would leave brown streaks on clothes in the wash. They used rainwater for laundry and shampooing and stuff."

"So what is a cistern like?" she asked.

Bodie gallantly deferred the question to Zach since he wasn't sure of the details himself.

"Big concrete tank, like I said. Maybe twelve, fifteen feet deep, eight or ten feet across. The top is usually a square of concrete with a hole in it, with a smaller circle of concrete over the hole for a lid. They had to have heavy lids so little kids couldn't open them and fall in. They usually have a ladder going down from the hole, so you can get in to clean them out. We've got a cistern at our place. Most old farmhouses do. They're expensive to fill in."

Bodie said, "I know the Silers have one. You know, Gracie, that milk can with the flowers in it, by the north wall. It sits on a round concrete slab. That's got to be the cistern lid."

"Are we going to open it?" Gracie asked, rolling over on her back to stick her skinny legs in the air.

"You bet. I figure it might take all three of us

to move that lid, so, Zach, you'll have to help. Okay?"

Zach nodded.

"Now, I'm out there every day working, and Gracie is usually there too, so we'll just keep our eyes and ears open, and when it looks like Henry and Althea are both going to be gone a while, we'll call you and you come over, and we'll open it up."

"Don't you think we should tell the police and have them do it?" Zach said doubtfully.

"Not yet." Bodie had pondered that point himself, and he was sure. "We don't have any hard evidence. You know yourself you have to have hard evidence or the police won't take you seriously. All we have right now are suspicions and theories. We have a missing Bella that nobody knows where she is except Henry, and he's not saying. We have Henry moving in some strange woman who he *says* is a relative, and whooping it up with her. And we have, oh, I forgot to tell you the best part. This morning Henry caught me looking around in the woods when I was supposed to be sawing, and he said to me, he says, 'I know what you're hunting, and you ain't going to find it up here.' Now if that's not a suspicious thing for him to say, I don't know what is."

"Well," Zach said slowly, "I still think we ought

to just tell the police what we know, or suspect, and let them do the searching."

Bodie shook his head. "Not until we have the body, buddy. They won't listen to us without hard evidence."

"What about cars? Do the Silers have a car that's missing?"

Bodie looked blank.

"They got an old junker," Gracie said. "I never saw them drive it, but they got it."

"What make, what year?" Zach shot at her.

"How do I know? Just a big old rusty car, kind of brown and tan, I think. Or maybe that was the rust. It looked kind of like Booxbaums'."

"Booxbaums'." Zach searched his mental car file. "That's an old Pontiac Firebird, '67 or '68. Is Silers' car there?"

Gracie said, "I don't know. I never noticed. They keep it in that old leaning-over garage between the house and the barn."

Bodie's spirits sank. The garage had been empty since he'd been working there. He remembered the open door, the empty blackness of the shed. Rats, he thought. Bella is probably alive after all. She drove away someplace in that car. There goes fame and herohood and girls looking at me with lust in their eyes.

But Gracie rolled over onto her stomach again and said in a high, firm voice, "He took that car off somewhere and hid it. Ran it into the river or something, so it would never be found. That way he could tell people Bella drove off in it."

Bodie's imagination kindled. "Of course. He'd wait a while, a few weeks or months, to let the trail get cold. Then he'd tell people he and Bella had split up and he didn't want to talk about it earlier because he was all choked up over it. Meanwhile, he's hidden the car, probably put a suitcase in it with her clothes, knocked her off, and dumped her down the cistern. Smooth as goose grease."

"I don't know," Zach said. "Trash a perfectly good car?" It would have been against his nature.

"Not a perfectly good car," Bodie argued with enthusiasm. "An old junker that probably barely ran and didn't have any trade-in value. And if it meant covering a crime, keeping out of the electric chair, that's what I'd do. Wouldn't you?"

Zach had to ponder loss of car against loss of life.

But Bodie was content. He knew how the murder had taken place. Now all he had to do was prove it and bask in glory.

The week passed day by day, as they usually do, but every day was an aggravation to Bodie. Henry simply refused to leave home. Each morning Bodie fed and watered the animals, retrieved eggs from old boots, and drove up into the woods, all with one eye on Henry or his pickup. Three times during the week Althea dressed up in town clothes and drove away, but never with Henry. Once Henry went to town on some errand, but Althea stayed home.

By Sunday Bodie was near desperation. Another five days and his job would be finished here. If things didn't start happening soon, Henry would get away with murder, and Bodie would have to go on being a non-hero.

Four afternoons during the week he and Zach had driven around the back roads, looking for a place big enough or a river deep enough to hide an old Plymouth. They found a long-abandoned '46 De

Soto, several patches of stinging nettle, and a couple of good places to park and make out, if either of them ever got lucky enough to need one. But no car that could have been Bella's.

On Sunday Bodie wasn't expected to cut wood, only to do the necessary animal chores. It was almost nine before he finished because he'd given himself an extra hour in bed. One of life's great luxuries, Bodie thought, was that of lying in bed after waking, just lying there remembering a dream, planning the day, and just relishing the soft sheets against his skin.

He put the feed bucket inside the barn, stopped to give Gloria a farewell scratch on the crest of her back, then started up the road toward home. A thought slowed his step. He went back into the farmyard, into the barn as though he'd forgotten to do something in case Henry was watching. Then he started toward home again, this time through Beauty's pasture.

As soon as the house was out of sight behind a line of trees, Bodie hunched down and began to circle back, keeping the barn between himself and the house.

Behind the barn, in the small lot at one side, was a huge manure pile made up of offerings from Gloria and the beef calves. Taking shallow breaths,

Bodie eased around the pile to stand just at the corner of the barn. From there he could lean out just a fraction and see Henry's back door and the pickup truck.

He checked his watch. Nine-fifteen. Church services in the Bacpane villages generally started at ten instead of eleven during the summer months, to avoid the heat. There was only a slim chance that Henry and Althea would both go to church today, but as desperate as Bodie was getting, slim looked a lot better than none.

Minutes ticked past. Bodie waited. Nine twenty-five. Nine-thirty. If it didn't happen in the next few . . .

The house door opened, and Althea emerged, wearing the same flowered dress she had worn last Sunday. Bodie held his breath.

She paused on the porch, turned, said something back into the house, then went on down the steps and across the grass toward . . . not her car! Hope sprang eternal in Bodie's breast. She levered herself awkwardly up into the passenger seat of Henry's pickup.

And there was Henry himself . . . hope flagged a little when Bodie saw that Henry was dressed in his everyday overalls, not church clothes. That might mean he was just driving Althea to church, not going himself. In that case, time was going to be critically short.

He turned and ran, leaping the edge of the manure pile almost successfully. Over the pasture fence, past Beauty, who grazed on oblivious to the drama around her. Over the far pasture fence and through the hayfield. Running was hard here. The ground was rough, and his feet kept turning.

At the creek he made his finest leap ever and only got one foot wet. And it was the same foot that hadn't quite cleared the edge of the manure pile, so that was all right.

Through the weed field he ran, braving burr and nettle for the sake of the cause. Across the backyard, over the sleeping dog and into the kitchen he plunged, breathless and wild-eyed.

Glenda and Boris stood just beyond the kitchen in the front hall, checking each other for turned-up collars and hanging slips. Gracie was just coming down the stairs looking like a female impersonator in her pink Sunday dress.

All heads turned toward Bodie.

"What's that stink?" Glenda asked.

Gracie, who was nobody's fool, said, "Is it time?"

Bodie panted, "Yes. Call Zach and come quick."

Mr. Tureen said, "Come to church with us, son. It's been a long time since we've all gone as a family. I like to show off my handsome children, you know. Hurry up and change, and we'll wait for you."

"Can't," Bodie panted, hanging onto the door frame with one hand and clutching his throat with the other. A week of woodcutting had failed to harden him to marathon fitness. "Sorry, Dad, Mom. Can't. Wish I could. Love to. But, can't. Got important job. At Henry's. Got to do. It now. Need Gracie to help."

"What is it?" Boris asked, instantly concerned. "Can't it wait till after dinner? I can help you then."

Bodie just shook his head, waved a hand in helpless apology, and turned to jog out again through the back door. Boris and Glenda exchanged questioning looks, and then they shrugged in unison. This was one of those times when it might be best not to know what the kids were up to, they decided wordlessly.

As Bodie leaped over Sport and down the back steps, he heard Gracie on the phone to Zach. Not a minute to waste if Henry was only driving Althea to church and coming right back.

He loped back toward Henry's through weed and wet, over clods and barbed wire. Yes, he decided. He would definitely have a legman to do all this stuff for him when he got to be a rich and famous detective.

The pickup was gone when he got back to the farmhouse, and so were Henry and Althea. Bodie called and knocked, just to be sure. Then he went around to the side of the house and stared at the cistern. This was it. The grand opening!

The concrete square was about five feet across and level with the ground. In the center was a disk of concrete eight inches thick and about two feet across, and centered atop this disk was an antique milk can two feet tall, filled with dirt and planted with marigolds.

Gracie came running from the direction of the road, being realistic about the matter of white tights and white shoes and pink dresses combined with weed fields and streams too wide to leap in a single bound.

"Got Zach," she panted. "He's on his way."

Her dress had little puffed sleeves and a smocked yoke. It was the kind of thing small girls were dressed up in, or mature women wore, attempting to look childlike and innocent. Gracie fell between two stools, so to speak, being neither child nor woman. With her boney brown face, her rooster-tail haircut, and her sunburned arms, the dress looked plain silly. But for some reason she had lately begun to like that dress and had more than once threatened to punch Bodie's lights out if he made any cracks about it.

"Here, help me with this," Bodie said, and grabbed one of the milk can's side handles.

Gracie took the other side, and together they rolled and wrestled the can off of the concrete disk.

Bodie knelt beside the disk, gripped it, tried to shove it aside. It didn't budge. Gracie threw her weight against it, ruining the knees of her white tights in the effort. The disk moved a fraction of an inch.

They were still shifting it by fractions when Zach drove in and came bounding toward them with a length of inch-thick rope in his hands. Wordlessly they looped the rope around the disk and leaned their three weights against it.

The disk scraped slowly aside, revealing first a sliver of black space beneath it, then a crescent, and finally a hole, two feet wide and black as the inside of a cow.

They stood silently looking down the hole. Far below Bodie saw a glint of water. A badly rusted iron ladder was bolted to the rim of the hole and disappeared from sight almost immediately.

Bodie looked at Gracie, at Zach. They looked expectantly back at him. It suddenly occurred to him that he was the leader of the expedition. He was the logical one to descend the depths, to reach into the icy black water. To touch with his own clean fingertips the dead and bloated and stinking flesh . . .

His stomach rolled over and quivered at the thought.

"Well," he said brightly, "ladies first."

"Hell no," Gracie said, backing away. "I'm not going down there."

No, of course he couldn't ask his baby sister to do something he was afraid to do himself. What kind of master criminologist would do such a thing? No man fit to call himself a man . . .

"What's the matter, Gracie," he taunted. "Are you scared to?"

"Of course I am," she said sensibly. "Who wouldn't be? That's a rusty old ladder that could break any minute; it's a deep hole with who knows how much water in the bottom, and a dead body floating around down there. I may be young, but I'm not crazy. You go down. This was your idea."

Bodie stared into the hole for another long moment. The light caught on something floating in the water. A hand? His stomach lurched again. He put his hand on the ladder and shook it. It felt tight and sturdy.

"I don't know," he said. "This ladder feels pretty wobbly to me. I doubt that it's safe for my weight. Zach, you don't weigh as much as I do. You go down."

Zach came forward and knelt to look into the blackness. His face lost a little of its color.

Bodie said, "You've probably been down in cisterns before, out at your place. You're the logical one to go down."

Zach just stared, mesmerized, into the depths.

Time ticked past. If Henry was just dropping Althea off at church, he could be back any minute. It grew painfully clear to Bodie that if anyone was going down to the watery grave, it would have to be him. Zach was transfixed, and Gracie had backed several yards away to stare with wary eyes.

"Okay," he said finally, "if the rest of you are too chicken." He forced himself to drop one leg into the hole. His toe found the ladder rung. He eased his weight onto that foot and began maneuvering the other leg over the rim of the hole. The ladder bore his weight without a tremor.

"Uh oh," he said, pulling himself up out of the hole. "I felt that ladder give a little bit. It's not going to be safe to climb down. Rats. I really wanted to get down in there and check it out."

Gracie relaxed and came close again, and natural color returned to Zach's cheeks.

"Well, I don't think there's a body down there anyway," Zach said. "If there was, we'd be able to smell it."

"After two weeks?" Gracie asked doubtfully.

They looked at one another, pooling their forensic ignorance. "Yeah," Bodie said finally. "You're right. It would still be smelly."

"Unless the water would do something to it," Gracie said.

A distant rattle caught their attention, gravel hitting pickup fenders.

"Quick," Bodie snapped. In a tangle of arms they got the rope around the cistern lid, dragged it back into place, and hoisted the milk can onto its perch.

When Henry drove up and alighted from the truck, the three of them were sitting like evil-free monkeys in a row on the concrete slab.

From the corner of his mouth Bodie muttered, "Let's test him. Follow my lead and watch for his reaction. Morning, Henry."

Henry stopped in surprise at the sight of them, especially at the sight of Gracie in a pink dress with puffed sleeves.

"What are you kids up to?" He sounded less

than happy to see them. Guilty? Worried? Bodie couldn't be sure.

"We were just sitting here on your *cistern*, Henry. I never noticed it before, but that's what it is, isn't it? A *cistern?*"

Henry glowered slightly, not an easy task for such a round, smooth face. "Of course it's a cistern. What'd you think it was, a swimming pool? Crazy town kids," he muttered.

Then, looking again at the group, he said, "What you doing here, Zach? How's come you're not helping your daddy put up hay, nice day like this?"

Zach blanked out, but Bodie's steel-trap mind came to the rescue.

"I called him, asked him to come over and take a look at Althea's car. I noticed you driving her to church this morning, so I figured there was something wrong with her car, and my friend Zach here is a whiz with auto mechanics. I just thought it would be a nice little surprise for you if we had it all fixed by the time you got back."

"Uh huh," Henry said slowly. "Then how's come you're all setting there on the cistern like a row of crows?"

Bodie thought again. "Well, we looked at the car and we couldn't see what the trouble was, so we thought we better wait and ask you about it when you got home." He smiled.

Henry didn't smile. "Uh huh," he said again. "You couldn't find the trouble."

He turned and looked toward the Chevy, which was parked in the sunlight just outside the leaning garage. The near front tire was flat as an ironing board.

Silence reigned in the little farmyard.

"Well," Bodie said with sudden briskness as he stood up. "Zach's specialty is really carburetors, Henry. There was nothing wrong with the carburetor. Come on, you guys, time to head for home."

They ran for Zach's pickup and drove off, leaving Henry shaking his head and muttering about damn-fool kids.

"Well, what did you think?" Bodie asked as soon as they were safely away. "Did you think he acted guilty or worried when we mentioned the cistern?"

"No," the others said in unison.

Bodie wilted. "Me neither. So, okay. That means he's hid her someplace else. All we have to do is find her."

"Sorry, buddy," Zach said. "We start cutting hay tomorrow. You're on your own."

Gracie was busy examining the bit of kneecap showing through the hole in her tights. No comment from that quarter.

Bodie sighed and slumped against the truck door. This was going to be a lonely profession.

10

For the next two days Bodie and Gracie redoubled their efforts to find the body. Time was running out, at least for Bodie. By Friday Henry's sling would come off, and Bodie's job, and the access it provided, would end.

While he did his feeding chores, Bodie searched the farmstead for possible hiding places in sheds and junk piles. In the woods while he looked for dead trees and fallen limbs with one eye, he looked for woodland graves with the other.

Meanwhile, Gracie in her unobtrusive way managed to cover every inch of Beauty's pasture and the adjoining orchard in a fruitless search for disturbed sod.

In the small snatches of time when he could get away from haying, Zach drove the most obscure back roads he could find, looking for an abandoned Plymouth. He walked the riverbank in every spot

ie knew of where a car could be driven up to the
bank and into the water.

"Zilch," he said to Bodie Tuesday night as they
sat on the Tureens' front porch steps watching the
sun go down. "And if you ask me, the whole thing
was a stupid idea. I'm not wasting any more of my
time looking for Bella Siler's car, and I think you're
crazy if you keep looking for a dead body of somebody who's probably not even dead."

Zach rubbed his toe along the spine of the dozing
retriever. With every rub Sport muttered a low
growl.

Bodie was revving up his arguments when he
saw his mother coming up the sidewalk. She'd been
at the neighbors, watching a videotape of a grand-
child in California taking its first steps and crying
into the camera.

"Watch out," Bodie whispered. "She's starting
on her Christmas jokes already."

Glenda's eyes lit when she saw Zach. She approached him with the relish of an uncontrolled
joke-teller with a virgin audience.

"Zach," she said, bearing down on him, "what's
green and mushy and festive?"

Bodie groaned, but Zach went along with her.
"Okay, what's green and mushy and festive?"

"Frog-nog!" she hooted. She climbed the steps

and went into the house laughing. Bodie and Zach exchanged looks but held in their hoots until she was out of earshot, not wanting to encourage her to come back and tell more.

The next morning while Bodie was feeding Gloria her Sow Joy and feeling sorry for himself for having to carry on the good fight without Zach, Henry appeared outside the pigpen fence.

"You don't need to cut wood today," Henry said. "I want you to clean out that calf pen instead. That'll take you most of the morning. And then tomorrow morning you can clean this one." He nodded toward the twenty square yards in which Gloria lived her porcine life.

Gloria's pregnancy was becoming bulgingly obvious, and Bodie supposed that Henry wanted the new arrivals to have clean earth under their little feet. Whoopee, Bodie thought as he looked around the pigpen. Gloom descended on his soul.

Well, that was tomorrow's job. Today's would be a shade less nasty. Cow manure was not roses in bloom, but anything smelled better than unshoveled pigpen.

Henry said, "You know where the wheelbarrow is, in the barn there, and you know where the shovels are. Manure pile is right behind the barn. You can't miss it."

Bodie snorted a wordless agreement to that.

The house door opened, and Althea's voice came chiming through the air, "Oh, Henry . . . I need you." Girlish flirtation lay thick on the words.

Henry grinned as foolishly as a boy and hurried away toward the house.

"Hah," Bodie muttered to Gloria, "you try to tell me there's no hanky-panky going on there. Hah. I wasn't born yesterday. I'm not blind. I didn't just fall off the turnip truck."

Gloria chewed her Sow Joy, looked up at him from beneath the tips of her ears, and kept her opinions to herself.

All morning while the sun grew hotter, Bodie labored in the calf pen at the side of the barn. He shoveled up chunk after chunk of calf manure into the wheelbarrow, then emptied the barrow onto the pile behind the barn and went back for more. The lot hadn't been cleaned all summer. It occurred to Bodie halfway through the job that Henry was using him to get a big unpleasant job done at minimum wage so he didn't have to do it himself. Two unpleasant jobs, counting tomorrow's cleaning of the pigpen.

When the last load was finally shoveled in and hauled and dumped, Bodie collapsed into the wheelbarrow himself, to sit and catch his breath for the walk home to lunch. He sat and breathed and looked casually at the manure pile. Then, with slowly tightening stomach muscles, he fixed his gaze on it.

The pile was roughly head high against the barn, sloping downhill from there, about fifteen feet long, six or eight feet wide. It was made up of loose mounds of cow and pig manure gathered through the years.

Suddenly Bodie knew. He knew where Bella's body was.

He came back to the farm after a quick lunch, came back with a foolproof plan to trap Henry. Simply offer to haul the manure pile away. Offer to haul it over close to the garden, where it would be handy to spread and dig into the garden earth, come fall. Henry would be startled; he'd cover it up but not before Bodie saw it. He'd make excuses why he didn't want Bodie to shift the pile. Then Bodie would be sure, sure enough to go to the authorities anyway. He'd act cool, so as not to spook Henry, but he'd hotfoot it to the police, get them out to the farm before Henry could relocate the body. And that would be it. The jig would be up.

On his way back to the farm after lunch, Bodie gloried in his sharp-wittedness. The manure pile was perfect for hiding a body. It was absolutely tailor-made. The loose dry manure was super-easy to dig into; the pile was plenty big enough to hide even a large body like Bella's, and best of all, it wouldn't show signs of the digging as earth in the woods or pasture would have. And besides, things rotted very fast in a manure pile, and even if there was some smell, who could tell with all the pig manure in the pile?

Bodie frowned for a moment and slowed his walk. If Henry did bury the body in the manure pile, would he take a chance of sending Bodie back there to work? Especially after what he said in the woods about "I know what you're hunting"?

Maybe. If the body was buried deep in the heart of the pile, there'd be no reason for Bodie to discover it. Nothing would show from the outside of the pile. And in fact, Bodie had been helping conceal it all morning with every new load he dumped onto the pile from the calf pen.

Or, Bodie thought as he had before, Henry might be one of those psychopathic killers who want to be caught. They hide their trails, but then call in clues to the police, or leave a message written in lipstick on the victim's bathroom mirror.

Thinking of Henry as a psycho killer didn't do Bodie any good in his attempt at cool as he climbed the back porch and knocked on the kitchen door.

Althea let him in. "Henry's in the other room," she said. "What did you want?"

Bodie shifted feet uneasily. "Well, um, I wanted to ask him if he'd like me to haul the *manure pile* for him."

The raised voice did the trick. In half a minute Henry came into the kitchen. "What's that about the manure pile?"

Bodie tried to study Henry's face intently while keeping his facial muscles relaxed and playing his part as not-too-bright neighbor kid.

"I said, I wondered if you'd like me to move that manure pile over by the garden for you. I noticed it was getting pretty high, and I just thought you'd like to have it over close to the garden."

Henry's eyes narrowed slightly. Bodie's hopes rose. They looked at each other for a full minute, both faces carefully expressionless.

Then Henry said, "I can't afford to pay you for no extra jobs like that. It'd take you a good three, four hours to shift that pile. I'm not going to pay you extra."

Bodie's mind raced behind his carefully held features. "Tell you what," he said finally. "I don't have anything else to do this afternoon. I'll just do it for you. For nothing."

Something shifted behind Henry's eyes, something watchful. "Why?"

Bodie shrugged. "Just doing you a favor." He thought, Now I've got my proof. I'll get out of here as fast as I can and get to town, to the police.

Suddenly Henry's face settled into a smile. "Okay, you're on."

"What?"

"I said, 'Okay, you're on.' Go on. Haul the manure pile for me. On your own time, no pay."

Bodie stared at him.

Henry smiled. "Maybe I'll just come along and watch."

This wasn't the way it was supposed to go, Bodie fumed as he began digging. Henry was just supposed to have shown so much guilt and shiftiness at the idea of having the manure pile moved that Bodie would know for sure that Bella was buried there. Then Bodie could have slipped away into town, got the police, let them do the digging, and that would be it. Now here he was, helplessly trapped into digging up the corpse while the insane murderer watched.

Everyone else seemed to be enjoying the afternoon. Gracie watched from her perch on Beauty, in the pasture just beyond the calf pen. And Henry brought a lawn chair from the porch and settled himself in the shade of a sprawling oak a few yards back of the manure pile.

Gracie hadn't been at home for lunch at the same time as Bodie, lunches being pretty casual in the Tureen house in summer. But Bodie had seen her on Beauty as he'd started around the barn with barrow and shovel, and he'd detoured over to her to whisper what was going on. She was poised to send Beauty galloping to town for help if the situation started looking dangerous, but with Gracie as his only safety net, he was not comforted.

Bodie shoveled with more scalp prickles than any manure-pile shoveler in the history of farming. At any moment the tip of the shovel might hit something soft and fleshy beneath the manure. The smiling farmer in his shaded lawn chair would become, on that instant, a psychopathic killer. And on that instant Bodie Tureen's life wouldn't be worth the manure at his feet.

He filled the barrow and rolled it with some difficulty around the barn, across the lumpy lawn, past the leaning garage and pigpen, then dumped it beside the vegetable garden and wheeled it back empty. The sun glared in his eyes and burned through his shirt and into his tender shoulder skin.

Another load and another. With each filled load Bodie shot a glance at Henry, who was now leaning back in his chair, half dozing.

Another load. Another. Shovel shovel, plod plod, dump and rattle and shovel some more.

After an hour or so Althea came around the corner of the barn with cans of Coke for herself, Henry, and Bodie. She brought another chair and a bag of crocheting and settled in for a pleasant afternoon. On his way back from his eleventh dump trip, Althea called Bodie over to show him the baby bonnet she was making for her neighbor's daughter's first baby.

Bodie shoveled on. He'd started in the middle of the pile since that was the most promising place for body burying, and he'd worked his way clear through to the barn wall and the ground. No body.

From that point the afternoon became almost unbearable. He was hot, he was achingly tired, he was sweaty and manure-stinky and overwhelmingly discouraged. Gracie abandoned her post and went home to sit in front of the air conditioner and read horse books.

"Why don't you go on back up to the house where it's more comfortable?" Bodie said finally to Althea and Henry.

Henry twitched awake from his nap. "Oh, I just

like watching another guy work," Henry said cheerfully. Althea smiled at him and started her next row of crochet.

It was five o'clock before Bodie finally wheeled the barrow into its parking place inside the barn door. His hands were raw with blisters, his arms were two feet longer than they were supposed to be from the weight of the barrow handles, and he had a painful sunburn coming on his scalp.

The manure pile was gone from the entire back length of the barn wall. Clean, bare earth lifted its pores to sun and air for the first time in decades.

Henry and Althea rose and folded their lawn chairs and started toward the house.

As he passed Bodie, Henry said, "Thank you, son. That was a nice favor you did me. I've been wanting to get that pile hauled for a long time; just never wanted to tackle the job myself. I'm obliged. Now, you best get Gloria fed and watered. I hear her calling for you."

Henry walked away toward the house, one hand riding gently on Althea's shoulder.

11

Bodie started for home that evening down a road that lengthened itself with every step he took. It seemed an impossible distance looking down that lonesome road, past Henry's orchard, past the Mulligans' house and fields, and on to the highway corner in the dim distance.

He had washed the worst of the manure off of his arms and bare legs beneath his cutoff shorts, but the stench of it was still in his shoes and in his heart. The hand blisters and muscle aches and sunburned scalp were bad enough, but disappointment and discouragement were even worse.

I need to go at this from a different angle, he thought as he trudged past the apple trees. I'm not having any luck finding the body, and I can't think of anyplace else on the farm that it might be. So maybe I'm chasing the wrong tail here. What would a master detective do?

Find out more about the victim? That's what book detectives do, to uncover hidden motives. Only, I already know who did it; I just can't find anything definite enough to take to the police. What can I do next? I've only got two more days before my job ends, and after that it's going to be almost impossible to go on with the investigation.

His trudges brought him close to the Mulligans' farmhouse, across the road from the Silers' orchard. As he approached, Bodie saw Emily Mulligan on her knees in the front lawn, jabbing at the underside of an overturned lawnmower.

Aha, he thought.

"Hi," he called, and veered across the grass toward her. "Having problems?"

Emily was a small, faded woman with the unsettling habit of staring hard into the eyes of everyone she talked to. She looked upside down at Bodie from under her armpit and managed to skewer his gaze, even upside down.

"Oh, Bodie. I picked up some baling twine, I guess. Got it wound around the blade, and she choked herself to death."

Bodie knelt beside the exposed blade of the little green Lawnboy and relieved Emily of her weapon, a small Phillips screwdriver. "Here, let me."

"I've been working over at Silers'," Bodie said although she hadn't asked. The mower job wasn't going to take more than a few minutes; best get onto the investigation as soon as he could. "Henry hurt his arm, you know."

"Yes, I heard. I see he's got his niece over there keeping house for him while Bella's away."

This is going to be duck soup, Bodie thought. "Yes, Althea somebody. She's very nice, very jolly. A big change from Bella, I'd say. Where did Bella go, anyway, do you know? I asked Henry, but he wouldn't tell me."

Emily's eyes sharpened like a hawk spotting a fieldmouse in the grass. "I don't know where she went. She never said a word to me about going anywhere, and Bella and I are very close. I thought she could have at least told me if she was going off on a trip somewhere. She's supposed to be my closest friend, after all."

Bodie was just about to say, "Do you think Althea is really Henry's niece?" when Emily said, "You've been working over there. What do you think? Is that woman really Henry's niece? The whole thing looks a little suspicious to me, if you want to know the truth. I was just wondering if you ever saw them, you know, acting . . . you know, suspicious."

Hey, whoa, Bodie thought. Who's pumping whom here?

He shrugged and stabbed a few more times at the twine embedded deep in the oil around the shaft of the mower blade.

"I don't know," he said. "I'm outside working. I don't really see them together all that much. But I did kind of wonder about it, especially since Henry is so zip-lipped about where Bella went to. I thought you might have some idea."

Emily gave a sour chuckle. "Heck, for all I know maybe she ran off with some other man. That Henry can't be much of a joy to live with. And I know Bella had an eye for men. Oh, not that she ever did much about it, you know what I mean. But you should have seen her after we got our new minister at our church. He is a good-looking man, I'll say that for him, and I could see maybe some of the younger women getting a little silly over him, but when a woman of Bella's age starts wearing sheer blouses and White Shoulders cologne to church every Sunday and volunteering for everything from Tiny Tot Sunday School class to janitor work practically . . ."

She ran out of breath and had to end with a knowing look, meant to convey worlds of unspoken meaning between two sophisticates stuck in a rural village.

Aha, Bodie thought again, with a triumphant jab at the twine tangle. Bella had the hots for the minister. Henry was jealous. He killed her in a fit of jealous rage.

"There," he said, standing up. "That should do it. Do you want me to start it for you, make sure it's running okay now?"

"No, no," Emily said, "I can do it later. Why don't you come in for a few minutes, have a cold drink or something? Tell me more about what's going on over at the Silers'."

"Well, no," he said modestly, "I really don't think I should do that. I mean, Henry is my employer and all. I probably shouldn't be gossiping about him. I was just kind of curious about where Bella might have gone to, that was all. I really didn't mean to get on the subject . . ."

"Have you been in the house? Can you tell if they're using separate bedrooms? Where has she got her clothes?"

Bodie backed toward the road. "Oh, uh, I don't . . . I never . . ."

Emily followed him. "Well, do they ever call each other pet names? Honey, darling, anything like that? Do they look at each other with feeling in their eyes?"

"No; I don't think . . ." He backed faster, stumbled over a tree root, scrambled to his feet.

"Well, you're right there with them every day. Don't tell me you work with your eyes closed, for heaven's sake. If Bella's getting cheated on behind her back, I have to know about it, Bodie. I am her best friend, after all. Who has a better right . . ."

He hotfooted down the road as fast as he could walk without the rudeness of actually running away from Emily.

She called after him, "If you see anything juicy going on over there, let me know."

Thursday morning. Only one more day left. Pressure mounted in Bodie as he carried Beauty her bathtubful of water, threw hay down for the calves, and poured corn into their feedbox. Frustration grew in him as he Sow-Joyed Gloria and played Find the Egg with the hens.

Only one more day after today, and Henry would be home free. He'd get away with murder because no one else thought there was a murder, except Zach and Gracie, and even they were beginning to lose interest in the whole thing.

He finished the chores and brought his intimate friends, the shovel and wheelbarrow, over to Gloria's pen. It was a much smaller pen than the calves', and it had a concrete base, so the job wouldn't be as long and hard as yesterday's. But the stench!

He'd gotten through two weeks of caring for Gloria by holding his breath or breathing shallowly through his mouth while he fed and watered her. That wasn't going to work now.

"Yo-o heave ho," he sang as the first shovelful rose and splatted into the barrow. He scooped again, this time coming up with an object half buried in the muck.

It looked like a shoe.

He tipped it out of the shovel and onto the grass outside the pen and looked more closely. It was a shoe, or rather a rubber overshoe, the kind designed to pull on over a woman's shoe.

For a long moment Bodie stared at the black rubber thing. His mind was stunned.

Now he knew.

He knew what happened to Bella Siler.

12

With a cagey glance toward the house Bodie picked up the overshoe with a stick and bore it away toward Beauty's pasture, where Gracie was squatted beside the horse's hind leg.

Having temporarily grown tired of sitting on an inanimate horse, she'd begun braiding things. Forelock and mane were already done up in crazily spiking pigtails. The tail was one fat long queue, and now she was making tiny braids in the fetlock tufts just above Beauty's hooves. The horse dozed on.

"I've got it!" Bodie called triumphantly. He held aloft the stick bearing the overshoe, as though it were the Olympic torch. "Look. I found this in the pigpen. You know what this is, don't you?"

Gracie stood up and examined the overshoe. "Looks like a stinky old overshoe to me. I remember Gramma Tureen used to have some like that. So what's the big deal?"

"The big deal is that I found it in the *pigpen*. Don't you get it? Pigs are omnivorous. They'll eat anything. Including flesh. Human flesh. Don't you get it?"

Gracie frowned, then stared horrified at him. "You mean Henry fed the dead body to his pig? Like that guy on Alfred Hitchcock?"

"Exactly. Only he didn't grind her up in the chicken feed."

Gracie's eyes widened till they seemed to cover her whole face. "What about her clothes?" she whispered.

"Gloria wouldn't eat clothes, I don't think. He probably went back afterwards and got the leftover clothes and got rid of them someplace; only this one overshoe had fallen off and got buried down in the manure, and he didn't see it. See?"

"So what are you going to do?"

He dropped his arm around Gracie's shoulder and said, "I'm going to confront Henry with the evidence and try to get a confession out of him. And you've got to help. When he realizes I'm on to him, he might try to hold me prisoner or something. I mean, he'd almost have to, to save his own neck. So my plan is two things. One, I'm just going to go barely inside the door. I won't ever let him get between the door and me. I notice that's the most common mistake guys make on television. They go into dangerous situations and let themselves get trapped because the killer gets between them and the door. So that will be my first safeguard.

"You are going to be my other one. I want you to stand outside the window and watch and listen, or maybe you better keep down. Don't try to watch or he might see you. Just listen outside that kitchen window, or whatever room they're in. If it sounds like I'm in trouble, run to the Mulligans' and call Dad. Got that?"

"Got it. What about Althea, Bodie? Do you think she's in on it with him? I mean, will it be two against one or what?"

Wisely Bodie said, "It'll be two against one either way, either them against me if she's in it with him, or else her and me against Henry if she's innocent. But the main thing is, I'm counting on you to run for help the minute you think I'm in trouble. No, don't wait that long. The minute he confesses. You run and get Dad and the sheriff as soon as you hear him confess. But don't make any noise. If Henry thinks he's safe, maybe I can keep him talking till the sheriff gets here."

As they started toward the house, Gracie whispered, "Bo, I'm scared. What if he kills you?"

"He won't. Don't worry." But the icy hand of fear was playing around in his intestines.

At the corner of the house they separated with a loaded meeting of eyes. Gracie bent low and disappeared into the bushes.

Holding the stick and its load of dynamite behind his back, Bodie knocked at the kitchen door. From inside he could hear the thrum of the washing machine in the basement and the cheering of crowds at a game show on television.

Henry appeared, looking disgruntled at the interruption. A red licorice bar was in his fist, a line of red at the corner of his mouth. For an instant it looked like blood to Bodie, and his heart almost quit on him.

"Well?" Henry said. "What you want? Did you finish mucking out the pigpen already?"

"Look what I found," Bodie said and with a flourish whipped the stick out from behind his back. His eyes stayed riveted to Henry's, watching for telltale guilty panic.

"What," Henry scoffed, "you found a stick?"

Bodie looked. The overshoe had fallen off, and he was holding forth a very ordinary stick of dead wood, two feet long, a finger thick, and smelling of pig manure.

"Oh. Well, um, wait a second . . ." Bodie retrieved the overshoe and held it up. "I found this. *In the pigpen*."

Henry looked blank. "So what? What are you bringing that smelly thing in the kitchen for?"

Bodie probed more keenly. "Who does it belong to, Henry?"

"Bella, I suppose. She had a pair like that. Just leave it on the back porch there and get back to work."

"*Had* a pair, you said. Hah. You slipped up one time too often, Henry Siler. I'm on to you."

The basement door opened, and Althea came up into the kitchen, a plastic laundry basket full of clean sheets in her arms. She hesitated and stared back and forth from Bodie to Henry.

Henry said, "I don't know what you're talking about, boy. But I'm paying you by the hour, so you'd best get back to your pen-cleaning."

Bodie's eyes became narrow slits. He held the overshoe with one hand and dropped the stick to grip the doorknob behind him with the other hand. "You know what I'm talking about, Henry. Don't play innocent with me. I've been on to you all along. I just didn't know where the body was. Now I know what you did with her. You fed her to the pig. And pretty soon the whole world will know, Henry. So don't bother pretending that you don't know what I'm talking about."

Henry look confused. "I *don't* know what you're talking about. On to me about what? Have you been out in the sun too long? Should I call your dad and have him come get you?"

"Don't make a move, Henry." He flashed his eyes toward Althea and saw that she was totally confused. Time to play his hand and get her on his side.

"Henry Siler, you murdered your wife and you disposed of the body by feeding it to your pig."

There. The words were out.

Henry's face looked absolutely blank for thirty seconds, then opened in broad laughter. "That's a good one, Bodie. You almost had me going there for a minute. Killed Bella and fed her to the pig. That's a dandy. Your mom would get a bang out of that one. Now get out of here and get back to work. It's almost time for 'Wheel of Fortune.'"

Henry turned and went back to the living room, smiling and chewing candy. Althea threw Bodie a look of confused disapproval, then bore her laundry toward the stairs to the bedrooms. Gracie's face rose into view at the window beyond the kitchen sink.

With her nose and forehead pressed against the screen, she looked disfigured and demented.

Bodie shrugged to her and shook his head. She cocked her head and weighed the situation for a moment, then dropped out of sight. In a minute he saw her heading back toward Beauty.

He was still standing in place when Althea came down again a few minutes later with a basketful of dirty clothes. Instinctively Bodie followed her down the steep narrow steps into the cellar.

It was a cellar typical of old farmhouses in the area, a very small dark square space under only the kitchen. Originally that one room had been the whole house. The other rooms were added later, but without basements under them. This room was dimly lit by one naked lightbulb hanging on a ratty cord from the ceiling and by a faint glow of daylight from one small high window near where Gracie had been standing. Shrubbery outside shaded out most of the daylight.

Only a part of the floor was concrete, a slab four feet wide along one side. The rest of the floor was dirt. On the concrete sat the washer and dryer and three upright cylinders that Bodie recognized as water heater, water softener, and well-pump pressure tank. The rest of the room was a dim clutter of junk; boxes of bottles and jars, a rusty spade, and several piles of magazines. The smell of rat droppings was thick in the air.

Althea busied herself with shifting loads from dryer to basket, washer to dryer, and basket to washer. Bodie sat on the stairs. He wanted to pump her for information, but for the moment he couldn't think of what to say. His mind was still reeling with his spectacular failure to wring a confession from Henry.

Althea said, "You were just kidding, up there, right? I mean, you don't actually think for one minute . . ."

In his master detective voice Bodie said, "You tell me, Althea. You tell me where Bella is."

She kept her back to him and made a production of pouring in a capful of detergent on top of the load of clothes in the washer. "Henry hasn't said where she is."

"He didn't tell you anything either? See? That's what made me suspicious in the first place. Nobody knows where Bella disappeared to. Nobody except Henry, and he's not saying. Doesn't that seem suspicious to you?"

"Well . . ."

"What did he tell you when he first called you and asked you to come down here?"

She closed the washer lid and set the dial, but

didn't start the machine and didn't turn to face Bodie. Instead, she talked at the wall. "He just called up one night and said would I like to come down and keep house for him for a while because he'd hurt his arm and Bella wasn't home."

"Just, she wasn't home? Did he say she'd gone away on a trip or what? What were his exact words? Try to remember."

"I can't remember." She turned finally and looked at him. "See, my husband died in May, and Henry, Uncle Henry, was probably feeling sorry for me, you know, wanting to give me something to do to keep my mind off my loss. You know. That's what I thought when he called. I wasn't thinking too clear, I guess. I never asked him about Bella. Oh, I did ask, I guess, when he first called. I said, 'Where's Aunt Bella?' but I honestly don't recall what he said. Something like 'She's gone for a while,' or some such. I figured maybe they had a fight and he didn't want to talk about it, so I never asked him again."

Bodie absorbed all that. Yes, he decided, it could have happened that way. Althea is probably in the clear. If she thought Henry and Bella had had a fight, she probably wouldn't ask too many questions about where Bella is or when she was expected back. Althea might be perfectly innocent about the whole thing, or . . .

"How did you tell me your husband died? I forget." He spoke as gently as he could.

She sniffled a little and said, "Corn picker got him."

Believable enough on the surface, he thought. Every fall the local news had at least one corn picker accident in which a farmer lost an arm or sometimes a life to the machine's vicious jaws. So it might have been a genuinely accidental death.

Henry and Althea might have been secretly in love for a long time, seeing each other at weddings and funerals and family reunions, keeping the glowing coals of their passion banked under a safety blanket of ashes. Then, suddenly, Althea's husband is dead, and only Bella stands in their way. Just get rid of Bella . . .

Or. Or it might have happened another way. A clue stood up in Bodie's mind and waved for attention. May is not autumn. May is not corn-picking season. What was Althea's husband doing getting killed by a corn picker in *May?*

The icy hand of fear clutched at his intestines again and shook them as hard as it could. Hairs rose on the nape of his neck as the realization washed over him. He was in a dark cellar with a sweet-looking little round-faced lady who may have killed her own husband. Upstairs, pretending to watch

"Wheel of Fortune," was a round-faced innocent-looking old farmer who had murdered once, if not twice, and who knew Bodie was on to him.

And here was Bodie, yards away from the door he'd planned not to leave. He was trapped with them.

And with no Gracie to go for help.

13

Cautiously he rose to his feet, measuring in his mind the distance up the stairs, across the kitchen, out the door to freedom and safety.

He could hear the television playing in the living room, but that was no proof that Henry was actually watching it. Of course he wasn't. He'd pretended to, as part of his cool, innocent act, but of course he would be crouching somewhere near the head of the stairs, listening to their every word, planning what to do with Bodie to shut him up forever.

The icy hand in Bodie's guts began tying knots.

His eye measured the window on the far side of the basement. He might be able to squeeze through it . . . or maybe not. Maybe he'd get hung up halfway through because his belly was too big, and then he'd be at their mercy for sure.

No, better to make a run for the kitchen door.

Althea was looking at him oddly.

"Well," he said, swallowing and trying to force a normal voice out through his lips, "guess I'd better get back to the pigpen. My work awaits."

She didn't say anything, just kept looking at him with her head tilted a little to the side.

Maybe Gracie had gone for help after all, he thought. She might have been just playing it cool herself, sauntering back toward the pasture. She might have taken off like a rocket once she got away from the house.

Or not. Better not count on it.

He backed up the stairs one cautious step at a time. It would be at the top that Henry would jump him if he was going to. Another step, another, then he turned and took the last treacherous step into the kitchen.

Henry loomed in the living room doorway, smiling a red-toothed smile.

Bodie bolted for the door, tripped over the stick he'd left lying there, and fell against the screen door and on out, onto the porch.

Henry came toward him.

Scrambling, terrified, Bodie half crawled, half ran across the porch, down the steps. Instinctively he chose the road rather than the hayfield. More public. Safer.

He ran like a wild animal, fists swinging, heart

pounding. The apple trees flashed past the corner of his eye. The Mulligans' house went blurring past the corner of his other eye. He was almost at the highway before he slowed enough to look back over his shoulder.

No one was chasing him.

Friday morning. Last day on the job. Bodie was glad. It was going to be hard to face Henry and Althea, he thought, walking up the road toward the farm.

He hadn't come back yesterday for evening feeding chores. After pondering the situation all afternoon, his thoughts on the subject of Henry and Bella were as clear as mud. Henry hadn't tried to kill him, tie him up, hit him on the head—any of the things you'd expect a killer to do to someone who was on to him. That could mean he was planning to get Bodie when he came back for evening chores.

Or it could mean he was innocent and Bella wasn't murdered, although Bodie's instincts all yelled against that possibility.

Or it could mean that Henry was bluffing it out, playing cool and innocent, secure in the knowledge that nobody was going to take Bodie seriously when he had no evidence.

Henry hadn't explained Bella's overshoe in the

pigpen. And he still wasn't offering any explanation for Bella's absence. That was the thing that kept sticking in Bodie's mind. If there was some innocent explanation of her whereabouts, why in the world wasn't Henry giving it?

Bodie thought about calling Henry and saying he wasn't coming. Henry's sling was supposed to come off that afternoon. He could manage the morning feeding and watering without Bodie's help.

But that would be the chicken way out, not the master detective's way. There was still a slim chance of cracking the case, he told himself as he approached the house on slower and slower feet.

There was still, also, the chance that he was going to his death.

Gracie hadn't come down to breakfast yet when Bodie left home, so he didn't know whether she was planning to come to the farm or not. He hoped so; she wasn't much, but she was more security than nobody.

Yesterday at lunch Gracie had asked what happened at Henry's after she left. She'd asked in a bored voice, as though she knew the answer wouldn't be very interesting. Bodie was still so confused about what had actually happened that he just said, "Oh, nothing," and left it at that.

As soon as the Siler house came into sight, Bodie

straightened up and quickened. Something was going on there. In the side yard, near the kitchen door, was a pile of junk that looked very much like the stuff he'd seen stored in the basement yesterday. He recognized one wooden shipping crate and a plastic trash bag full of empty bottles.

While he stood at the edge of the yard trying to figure it all out, Henry came out carrying another armload of junk.

"What are you doing?" Bodie asked.

"None of your business. You don't work here anymore," Henry said. He pulled some money from his overalls pocket and tossed it toward Bodie. Several twenties, it looked like.

Bodie raked the money off of the grass and stuck it away in his pocket before he said, "Are you firing me?"

"You could say that. You didn't show up last evening for chores. And you said some pretty hateful things to me yesterday, Bodie Tureen. I thought you was kidding at first, and I laughed them off, but then when I thought about it some more, I realized you was dead serious. You actually accused me of doing in my wife. That's a downright insult where I come from, boy. I don't want to see you around here, ever again, and that goes for that sister of yours, too."

So that was it. This was Henry's solution to the problem of Bodie Tureen. Fire him, get him off the place, keep on acting like the injured innocent. Then, if Bodie tried to make trouble for him, it would look like simple spite. The kid got fired, so he's going around spreading vicious lies about poor old Henry.

Damn clever, Henry Siler. Good move. Only it won't work.

"Okay," Bodie said pleasantly. "But I'll go ahead and do the morning chores since I'm already here."

"No need. Althea and I already done them."

"Ah." Bodie nodded, stalling for time. "Uh, what are you doing, cleaning the cellar?"

"None of your business."

"Oh. Well. Sure, okay, be seeing you, Henry."

He turned and walked away down the road, intending to circle back through the shelter of the orchard trees, back to the barn where he could creep up to the garage or henhouse, someplace close enough to watch the house. Something was happening there this morning. All of his instincts were agreed on that.

He started down into the ditch to climb the orchard fence but hesitated as a truck rumbled past. He didn't want to be seen climbing private fences.

It was a cement truck from Ajax Ready-Mix, the kind of truck with the huge turning drum mounted on the back for mixing and pouring large amounts of cement.

Bodie hesitated at the fence, watching the truck as it slowed at Henry's lane and turned in.

A cement truck. Somehow that cement truck jangled his detecting instinct.

A picture flashed in his mind: a dim, rat-smelly cellar, trash heaped in dark corners and . . . a spade leaning against the wall.

And now, a cement truck.

Suddenly Bodie knew, absolutely and without a doubt, where Bella Siler's body was.

14

Easy now, play it cagey, he told himself as he slunk
from tree to tree through the orchard. You've made
a fool of yourself too many times already in this
Bella business. This time, do it right. Get your facts
first before you get other people involved.

He moved through the long grass of the orchard,
keeping trees between him and Henry, who was
standing beside the cement truck talking to the
driver and pointing toward the cellar window.

No time to lose. At the corner of the barn Bodie
crouched low and began a waddling duck-run that
hurt his thigh muscles unbearably. He circled behind the barn, the machine shed, the chicken house,
then made a brave dash across the open space of
the backyard to the cellar window.

If Henry turned away from his conversation with
the truck driver, he would see Bodie right there,
just yards away from him. But he didn't turn.

His heart thudding, Bodie knelt at the window, shaded his eyes with his hands, and looked inside.

There it was. There, in the dim glow of the light bulb, was Bodie's proof: a dirt-crusted spade. A shallow grave just in front of the clothes dryer.

And beside the grave, partly inside a black plastic trash bag, was a tangle of white objects. A skeleton, heaped in haste upon itself. Not the full-fleshed body he'd been searching for, but the skeleton of it. How long does it take, he wondered fleetingly, for a body to become a skeleton? Then there was no more time to think.

Without looking toward Henry, who was still talking, Bodie scrambled to his feet and did his crouch run, back around the buildings. Near the pasture fence he saw Gracie wading toward him through the hayfield, eating a breakfast banana as she walked.

As he ran, the whole thing became clear in his mind. Henry had fed his wife to the pig, but Gloria hadn't eaten the bones. The bones and that telltale overshoe. And as soon as Henry knew Bodie was on to him, he decided to bury the rest of the evidence in the cellar, under the new cement floor. Bodie had caught him in mid-transfer.

Bodie grabbed the fence post and did a movie-style flying leap over the barbed wire.

Almost over.

Pain shot through him in a place he couldn't grab in front of a younger sister. Hobbling now, he half ran across the pasture, around Beauty, who wasn't moving for anybody, and toward the far fence that Gracie was climbing. Carefully.

"Gracie, go quick. Get help. I know where the body is. I've *seen* it. Get the police quick, or it'll be too late. Quick!"

Somewhat slow on the uptake, she said, "What? Where? Where is it?"

"He's burying her skeleton in the cellar, under the dirt floor, stupid," he almost shouted. "Cement truck's here. They're going to pour cement right over where her bones are going to be buried. So hurry!"

Once she understood, Gracie was as game as the next guy. "I'll take Beauty. That'll be fastest. Give me a leg up, and open the pasture gate."

"You haven't got a bridle or anything," Bodie wailed.

"That's okay, I can handle her. Get the gate."

He tossed Gracie up onto Beauty's back, opened the wire pasture gate, then ran toward the house. He'd wasted too much time already.

Henry and the cement-truck man were standing close together, looking at the cellar window, when

Bodie ran up. The cement man, ignoring Bodie, began unloading sections of metal chute and setting them up between truck and window.

"Wait, stop," Bodie yelled at him. "You can't pour cement down there."

The man stepped calmly around Bodie's flailing arms and said, "Yep I can. Chute'll fit through the window, no problem. Pour the stuff right down onto the floor."

"No, no, you don't understand. There's a skeleton buried down there. He killed his wife and buried her under the dirt floor, and now he wants you to cover it with concrete so nobody can ever find it."

The man paused and looked across Bodie at Henry. Henry smiled a crooked smile and made a circle near his temple with his finger. Crazy kid.

"No. Listen. Just wait. The police are on their way. My sister went for help."

All three of them turned to look toward the pasture. Beauty stood just outside the gate snatching at the fenceline grass while Gracie's legs flailed helplessly.

The two men looked at each other and nodded agreement. The kid was crazy.

"You go down to the cellar and finish moving things out of the way," the cement man said to

Henry, "and be sure the end of that chute is lined up where you want it."

Henry disappeared into the house.

"No, really. Listen. I'm not crazy," Bodie pleaded. "He really did murder his wife. You could be arrested for obstruction of justice if you don't wait till the sheriff gets here."

Bodie looked helplessly toward Gracie, who had managed to drive the horse six or seven feet along the fence.

"Gracie," he shouted, "get off the stupid horse and run for it."

Now the cement man was throwing levers on the truck, unrolling a hose and walking it toward the water faucet at the back corner of the house.

Gracie was kicking and slapping as hard as she could. Beauty moved forward three more steps, into the hayfield. There, in a horse heaven of ripe alfalfa, her head dropped again.

Suddenly the giant drum atop the truck bed began to turn and rise as water from the hose poured into it, along with sand and dry cement from the truck's holding tanks. The cement man climbed to the top of the truck bed to regulate his levers.

"Listen. You've got to believe me," Bodie pleaded.

"Why?"

"Why?" The question was rather a stopper. "Be-cause . . . because I'm right. Henry is a murderer, and you're helping him get away with it."

"Uh huh. Look, would you grab that second section of chute there and give it a shove to the left? It's a little bit out of line."

Bodie gripped the chute, started to shove, then said, "No, I won't. What am I doing helping you when you're helping him?"

Another glance toward Beauty showed him that Gracie had finally wised up and abandoned the speed and drama of a horseback rescue and was running full tilt across the hayfield on her own legs.

Good. Five minutes for her to get to the house and call Dad and the sheriff. Five minutes or less for Dad to get here, maybe longer for the sheriff, or shorter, depending on where he was in his patrol car when the call came in.

"All I have to do is stall him that long," Bodie thought, and promptly shoved over the whole chute.

"You stupid kid," the cement man bellowed. "I said give it a little shove to straighten it out. I didn't say knock the whole thing down. Stupid kid. Get out of the way."

He came down off the truck and began reassembling the corrugated steel lengths that made up the slide-like chute from truck to window.

Pretending to help, Bodie got in the way as much as possible, kicking over the metal support leg under the first length of chute and generally waving his arms around as irritatingly as he could.

Through the window came Henry's voice. "What's the holdup out there?"

Althea's head appeared in the kitchen window.

"Nothing," the cement man yelled back. "Just this stupid kid trying to help and screwing everything up. Is he yours? Why don't you tell him to get lost. I'm trying to get a job done here."

"Nah, he's not mine," Henry called back. "I've been trying to get rid of him myself."

"That's because I'm on to him," Bodie panted. "Please, just hold off till the sheriff gets here."

"Look, kid. I don't know you from Adam, but I go to the same church as Henry Siler, and I ain't listening to any of your wild talk about him being no murderer. I've got to pour three yards of concrete here, get it dressed off, and be up to Gorham by noon. So get out of my road."

The chute was back in place.

"Did you get your stuff moved?" the cement man called to Henry.

"Let 'er rip," Henry called.

"No," Bodie wailed.

The roar of the turning drum changed pitch, and a trapdoor at the top of the chute bulged open.

Bodie flung himself onto the chute, gripping its sides and struggling upward toward the trapdoor. He was like a small child trying to climb up a long and slippery slide. His knees slipped. He fell flat.

Down upon him came the slow-moving river of concrete, thick and gray and gleaming.

He shut his mouth just in time.

Turning his head and squeezing his eyes shut, he felt himself being pushed down, down . . .

He splayed out his feet and caught himself against the window frame, and held on for dear life.

Cement poured over his head, down his collar. It spilled over the edges of the chute onto the ground.

Through the racket came the sound of a slamming car door. Help, at last!

Through one squinted-open eye, Bodie saw Henry walking past, fast. Making his getaway.

With a superhuman heave Bodie rolled off of the chute and staggered after Henry, slowed by the heavy globs of cement running down his body and into his shoes. His eyes were half shut from the stuff, so he could see only the bottom half of Henry, but it was enough.

With a wild yell and a clumsy flying tackle,

Bodie hurled himself at the escaping Henry. Henry stopped; Bodie slid down the length of Henry's body with his slippery arms still around Henry's ankles. Triumph swelled in his cemented breast. He'd done it!

He opened one eye and saw . . . a woman's shoe.

Two of them. Big ones. Above them were a pair of fence-post legs in support hose, and above them . . .

Bella Siler.

15

Things happened fast at that point, like film on fast-forward. While Henry was losing his balance from being hobbled by Bodie's arms and falling onto Bella, who staggered backward and sat, quite hard, on the ground, Boris Tureen drove in with the photographer from the paper. Both of them leaped into the action, Boris waving his arms and the photographer shooting. Glenda popped up out of the back seat of the car and ran to Bodie yelling, "My baby, my baby, what are they doing to you?"

Althea called from the porch steps, "My heavenly days, what is all this racket?"

A siren stitched through the noise as the sheriff's car roared in. The cement man got his chute back in order and bellowed that he had to be in Gorham by noon. He threw the gears on his truck, restarting the roar and ka-thud of the drum that mixed the wet cement and sent it sliding down the chute unhampered by bodies of boys.

When he recognized Bella, Bodie just rolled over on his back, released Henry's ankles, and moaned.

"What's going on here?" the sheriff demanded. "We had a homicide report. Who is the deceased?"

Wordlessly Bodie lifted a cement-frosted arm and pointed at Bella.

"What *is* going on here!" Bella demanded. "Henry, what on earth . . . ?"

"The kid is off his nut," Henry yelled, struggling to his feet with the help of Boris and Glenda. "He's out of his tree. The light's on upstairs but nobody's home. His elevator doesn't go all the way to the top floor. Get him off my property. Get him away from me."

Bodie climbed to his feet since lying there wishing for death wasn't getting him anywhere. "I'm sorry, Henry. I guess I made a little mistake."

"A little *mistake* . . ." Henry lunged for Bodie's throat. Hammerlocks from Bella and Boris held him back, but only barely.

Two more figures joined the lawn party, Gracie, who was very sweaty and dirty and limping piteously, and Althea who said, "Bella, welcome home. I didn't hear you drive in over all this racket.

I've got the coffeepot on. Come on inside. Did you see Henry's surprise? He's getting your basement floor cemented for you. Isn't that nice?"

"Wait a minute," Bodie bellowed after them, but they ignored him and went into the house for coffee.

"All right now," the sheriff said in his toughest sheriff voice, "somebody tell me what's going on here. Boris?"

Boris shrugged and looked bewildered. "Darned if I know. Gracie called the office a little bit ago and said to get right out here, Bodie was being held prisoner by a mad murderer. So naturally Glenda and I came right out. I mean, most parents would, wouldn't they?"

Glenda had taken a fistful of Kleenex out of her shoulder bag and had managed to get them stuck in Bodie's fast-drying armor of gray cement-mud while trying to wipe it off his cheek.

"We've got to get this boy under water," she yelled, bouncing from foot to foot and making bare-handed swipes at the globs of hardening cement on Bodie's chest and legs.

"He's not moving until he tells me what's going on here," the sheriff insisted.

"Then he'll never move again!" Glenda grabbed Bodie's elbow and dragged him toward the side of the house. Ignoring the frantic yells from the cement man atop his truck, she unscrewed his hose from the tap on the house wall and shoved Bodie to his knees under the gush of water.

The sheriff followed. "All right, young man, start talking, and this better be good."

Henry followed them to the side yard, and the photographer followed Henry, still shooting. Gracie hobbled to her mother and whined, "I hurt my foot. I hurt my foot. I was the one that went for help, don't forget."

Bodie emerged from the waterfall very wet and mostly de-cemented, and stood up with as much dignity as possible under the circumstances.

"Hook that water back up," the cement man bellowed. "You're throwing off my mixture. This is the craziest job I ever did, and I'm charging double for labor." He aimed that last at Henry.

Bodie tried to think what a master detective would do in a situation like this. He couldn't think of a single master detective who would be likely to end a case by being shoved under a water faucet by his own mother.

"I thought he'd killed his wife," he said in as reasonable a voice as he could muster. "See, I came to work for him a couple of weeks ago, and he wouldn't say where his wife had disappeared to, and he was acting suspicious, so I—so my friends and I started looking for the body. That's all. It's perfectly simple. And I saw the skeleton. I saw a skeleton," he repeated hopefully. "Henry was burying a skeleton in the cellar floor. So when I saw that he was going to pour cement down there, I naturally sent for help. Go see for yourself. There's a skeleton!"

"Skeleton," Henry bellowed. "I'll give you skeleton." He stomped into the house and came out a minute later with a black plastic trash bag, which he emptied onto the grass.

Bones.

Grunting at the effort of bending over, Henry laid out the bones in the shape of . . .

"Perfection," Henry said when he could get his breath.

"Your pig?" Bodie said, dismayed.

"Not just a pig, sonny. That was the greatest Hamp sow ever bred in . . ."

Gracie's cackle split the air. "Henry, you buried your pet pig in your cellar?"

"It was winter when she passed on," Henry said defensively. "The ground was froze outside. What else could I do? I always meant to relocate her; I just never got around to it. Remembered at the last minute after I ordered the cement."

Bodie stared down at the skeleton. It was a pig,

no doubt about that. But still, there were things that didn't add up here.

"Why didn't you tell anybody where Bella was?" Bodie asked. "You could have avoided the whole thing if you'd just told somebody, anybody, where she was. Even her best friend didn't know where she was. You've got to admit that looked suspicious."

The group became suddenly very quiet. Everyone looked at Henry, who opened his mouth to yell at Bodie. No yell came out. He looked toward the kitchen window, where Bella and Althea watched through adjoining screens as they drank their coffee.

"Oh, you might as well tell them," Bella said finally. "I can see there's going to be no peace around here till you do. Honest to Pete, all I wanted was a little privacy for once."

Henry said, "She was off having otoplasty. She made me swear I wouldn't tell anybody, not even Emily or Althea. I kept your secret, honey pie, didn't I?"

He threw that last toward the window, and Bella beamed down at him.

"Yes, you did. You were very good. Except for all these licorice wrappers I see around the house."

Bodie shook his head to clear it. "What the heck is . . . what did you say?"

"Otoplasty," Henry said. "Plastic surgery to get

her ears flattened back. See, she's always had ears like jug handles, and it always bothered her. She thought they took away from her beauty. I said they never, but you know how women are about things like that. So I told her if Gloria's spring litter was ten or more piglets, we could afford for her to go have it taken care of. They take a little tuck right back in here, behind the ears." He demonstrated on his own woolly ears.

Bodie's lightning mind was skimming back over the past two weeks. "But, Henry, that time up in the woods. You said, 'I know what you're hunting, and you ain't going to find it up here.' What did you mean by that if you weren't talking about a buried body?"

Henry stared at him. "Ginseng, of course. I figured you were hunting ginseng beds. Every fall I get ginseng hunters up in those woods, and they never find any."

"What's ginseng?" Gracie asked.

Boris said, "A valuable plant that grows wild in the woods some places. The roots sell for a lot of money."

"Well, wait a minute," Bodie said. "What about Bella's overshoe in the pigpen? How do you explain that?"

From the window Althea said, "I borrowed your

overshoes one day, Bella. Henry asked me to take the table scraps out to the pig, and I put on your overshoes, and then one of them came off in the muck, and I didn't want to pick it up. Bodie was nice enough to bring it back for me."

"Well, why didn't you say so?" Bodie bellowed.

"You didn't give me much chance, what with all your murder accusations, dear. I was so shocked about that, I completely forgot about the overshoe."

Bodie's mind scrambled for one scrap of justification. "Then how did Althea's husband get killed on a corn picker in *May?*"

There was a long silence, then Althea said, "Why Bodie, surely you didn't think . . . why, my husband wasn't a farmer; he was an implement salesman. That picker got away from him while he was demonstrating it to a buyer, that's all. Shame on you for your thoughts."

The sheriff said, "So in other words, no one has been murdered here, right?"

He snorted and drove off in a huff, almost colliding with Zach's father's pickup, which came roaring into the yard. Zach leaped out and came running.

"I got here as fast as I could after Gracie called," he puffed. "Did you get him?"

The photographer took his picture. Startled but willing, Zach posed. Boris said, "Quit wasting our film. There's no story here. Come on, Glenda, we better get back to the office."

Zach watched their departure, then turned back to Bodie and said, "What happened?"

Bodie opened his mouth to answer, but had no words. It was Gracie who said, "We found Bella's body. But she was still using it."

The three of them rode home in Zach's pickup, with Grace in the middle and Bodie mashed against the door handle. The small pain in his rib was nothing compared to the black death-wish cloud that smothered his soul.

Brightly Zach said, "Just think, old buddy, someday you're going to laugh about all this. It'll make a great story to tell your grandchildren."

"What grandchildren? Nobody's ever going to marry me after this humiliation. Here I thought I was going to be this super-hero and have girls climbing all over me because I solved the big murder mystery. Hah."

He sank lower in the seat.

"Look at it this way," Zach said. "You earned the money you wanted, you got a couple of weeks of good hard exercise, and I can tell you've lost a few pounds around the middle there. You've hardened up. And we had fun, didn't we?"

Bodie looked unconvinced but he surreptitiously

pinched a roll of stomach. Was there more muscle in there, less fat?

He thought back over the past two weeks. "We did a good investigation, didn't we? Nothing wrong with the way we did our investigation. It wasn't our fault Henry hadn't killed her. And one skeleton would look pretty much like another in that dim a light. I never did get a good look at the skull, only the leg bones and ribs."

Gracie cackled, then threw her head back and laughed hard, slapping her leg and leaking tears from her eyes. "That old guy *buried* his *pig* in his *cellar*. And he called *you* crazy. It's like that joke of Mom's, about the guy who ate his pig one leg at a time."

No one could hear Gracie laugh without joining in. Zach roared, and finally Bodie rolled down his window, stuck his head out into the hot river of air, and laughed along with them.

Life began to seem less dead-ended. He might survive this humiliation, he thought, even though the story would be all over town before noon. He might survive if he kept his sense of humor, so that people laughed with him, not at him.

Possibly there could even be a girl for him one day in the future. He might have to settle for one who spit in her sister's hair, though.

Ah well, he sighed.